FUNCTIONAL
FAMILIES

FUNCTIONAL FAMILIES

Stories By

Taylor García

ACKNOWLEDGEMENTS

The following stories have appeared previously in literary journals: "Bird Dog," in *Fifth Wednesday Journal*; "Tiffin at Duckworth's," in *Diverse Voices Quarterly*; "Working On It," in *Hawaii Pacific Review*; "My First War," in *Jelly Bucket*; "Power Hour," in *Chagrin River Review*; "Bat Out of Hell," in *Driftwood Press*; "Monica in Georgetown," in *The Writing Disorder*; "Agony in the Garden," in *Evening Street Review*; "Wheel of Fortune," in *Litro*; "Aphrodite's Island," in *Caveat Lector*; "Highway Dark," in *The Griffin*; "The Big Night," in *Adelaide*; "Sad Last Days," in *Umbrella Factory*.

Thank you to the editors of the fine literary journals cited above for having faith in my writing and bringing my stories to your readers.

Thank you to all my friends and mentors for your support and friendship while at the Pacific University Oregon MFA program. Notably, the Kool Kids: Shaun Hayes, Randy Simons, and Mark Young for being my first writer bros, and to Larry Feign and Karen Ackland, for great conversations about books, writing, and life. To Pam Houston, who taught me to slow down and put some skin on the skeleton's bones, Laura Hendrie, for helping me go back to basics in order to get better, Brady Udall for reminding me to put myself in the story, and to Jess Walter for your encouragement, wit, and guidance.

To Steve Almond, who inspired me to keep writing: thank you for teaching me mercy. To Josh Goldfaden, an early writer lifeline, rest in peace always. Thank you to Susan Lawson for always lending your editorial and proofreading expertise, and to *mi hermano* Jeremy Lawson, you will always be my I.R.

Many thanks to the crew at Writer's Relief for your professionalism and perseverance.

To my large, loud, and loving family—*mi familia,* thank you truly. You are my favorite audience and my biggest fans.

And to my number one, mi Bonita, and our Pancho and Sancho, thank you for having patience with me and for letting me go to these worlds I inhabit in my mind and on paper. Your love inspires me always.

Sincerest thanks to the amazing people at Unsolicited Press who brought this collection to life, especially: S.R. Stewart for your kindness and professionalism, Jay Kristensen Jr. for your fine editorial skills and guidance, and Kathryn Gerhardt for your artistry.

For my family.

Contents

Preface

As far as we know, our people have been in the state now known as New Mexico since the 1600's, when the region was called Santa Fé de Nuevo Mexico, a remote northern province of then New Spain. And by *our people*, I mean my family, the descendants of the mestizos of the region—the mixed blood offspring of the first waves of Spanish immigrants to the area and the indigenous peoples of the American Southwest. These early agrarian settlers of New Mexico were neither Native American, purebred Spaniards, nor Mexican quite yet, however their cultural identity as racial hybrids would remain a constant, while their national identity would shift over time based on which flag flew over the land. New Mexico's status as a province of New Spain ended in 1821 as a result of Mexico's independence from Spain, making the area a Mexican territory up until 1848, when, by way of the Mexican-American War, the United States gained control of New Mexico.

Multi-generational New Mexicans have therefore suffered from a centuries-long identity crisis. What *are* we exactly? One logical label is Neomexicano, a sub-identity within the larger North American Hispano heritage. We are, in effect, our own off-shoot of a people that are not quite Native American, Iberian European (i.e. Spanish), or Mexican, yet we are indeed a blend of all three. And so goes my origin story, the one that creeps up every time I complete a demographic survey. Which bubble do I fill in?

In Latin American/Hispanic culture, name is often a key indicator of who you are. Within my lineage, there is one anomaly amongst all the Spanish surnames in the pedigree:

Taylor, my real "sur"-namesake. My great-great grandfather was an English immigrant who found his way to the New Mexico and Colorado region, where he met my great-great-grandmother Trujillo and started the Taylor family. On the other side of my family, one name has remained a constant since 1825: García. My great-great-great grandfather García was himself the essence of a simple Northern New Mexican farmer living in the heart of northern native New Mexico.

Who these men really were, my grandfathers Taylor and García, is mostly lost to history, but it is here, with their names combined to form my pen name as a means to honor my heritage, that I present these stories of which many are snapshots of mixed cultures, identities blended of two, sometimes three, distinct worlds.

FATHERS

BIRD DOG

DAD'S SITTING NAKED at the kitchen table, covered only by a white lacy shawl. His forehead glistens with sweat and he stares out the window, pouting. He has the old floor vents on full blast, and I'm surprised he's not dead from the heat. It's a typical Santa Fé summer evening, still well into the eighties. I shut off the furnace and throw open a couple of windows.

"Heater's on again, Dad. It's August. Remember?"

"Get out of here, you bastard," he says.

"Dad, it's me. Reynold. Your son."

He grabs the ends of the shawl and wraps it tighter around himself. He turns away from me and sticks up his nose. Today he's Mercedes Madrid. She's the mean one.

"Come on, Dad, take that damn thing off."

"I'm waiting for José," he says.

"I'm not sure he's coming. Now get up. Let's get some pants on."

His gut has grown in the last year, rounder and lower, but his legs and arms are still skinny as ever. His years spent in tanning beds and under the high desert sun have kept him brown, though it's turning grayish now. Ashy.

"José said he'd be here at twelve noon. Damn him all to hell."

"There's no José, Dad. Come on." I reach for him. "What's burning? And why does it smell like piss?"

He has the Magic Chef cranked to 450. Inside, a pair of his white undershorts—one of the men's garments he still

14

wears—lies flat on the top rack, placed with care, the ends stretched out. They're yellowed and just starting to smoke.

"Why'd you put your damn shorts in the oven, Dad? Has Marjorie been here?"

I twist the dial back, grab some tongs, and pull out the shorts. They smolder under cold water, and I fling open the window above the sink to let the stink out. Weeds poke up from the flower box that hangs on the windowsill where Steve's petunias used to grow and where a spider has taken over. Dad hasn't been outside in a while. It's better if he stays indoors.

His smug face makes me want to hurt him. It's the same face he wore in court for his and Mom's divorce. Steve, who back then we thought was only his best friend, waited outside the courtroom and turned away when Rob and I walked out, holding Mom. The way Steve went for Dad, helped him out of the building, everything made sense.

"I'm drying my lingerie," he says. "For my date."

"God damn it, Dad, this isn't lingerie. You're roasting your fucking underwear."

"Who are you?"

I grab his shoulders and turn him toward me. His nakedness always shocks me. Marjorie calls more these days, needing my help. She can't seem to do it alone, especially since he's abandoned clothes. He's slipped further since I was here last week. He's more eight-year-old boy than eighty-two-year-old man.

"Okay, Mercedes. Listen: there is no José, you are not going on a date, and you do not put your shorts in the oven to dry them."

He hums a tune I remember him singing when I was little. The words are something like, *Johnny he's a joker, he's a bird.*

15

He doesn't budge. I leave him there to find a robe and decide it's time to fire Marjorie. I dial Rob. He's never in the mood to talk about Dad, but maybe today he'll have some sympathy.

"It's getting worse. Maybe we should put him in a facility." I grab Dad's robe from the hallway bathroom.

"Whatever you say," Rob says.

"You do have a say in the matter."

"No, not really. You're the executor," Rob says.

Rob holds onto the idea Dad loved me more. He teases me to this day about it, says I'm in charge because I was our fairy father's favorite. Really, it was the state. Three years ago, APS called me after Mrs. Rogers next door called them. Steve had passed away the year before from a battle with lymphoma, and it wasn't too long before Dad started to slip. The day I got the call, Dad had wrecked his shopping cart into Mrs. Rogers at Albertsons. He was in heels and screamed at her. The state later named me executor.

That's what I get for being four minutes older.

"Why do you go through all the trouble, anyway? You're not getting a dime of his money," Rob says.

"His money's going to his care. He needs *someone*, Rob."

"Like I said: whatever you want to do is fine."

In the late part of the summer after Rob and I finished college, we sat for the last time as a family at the dinner table, but we didn't eat. Mom and Dad told us they were getting a divorce. Mom's face was a permanent purple from all the crying, and Rob was the only one who addressed the issue head on. He said he never wanted to speak to Dad again and had no love for a cheater, even though they hadn't told us why, or if there was any cheating going on at all. Rob wished Dad a long lonely life, then he got up and left. That very second, everything fell on me.

"Thanks for your input," I say. "I'll remember not to ask you again."

"You're welcome," Rob says. "How's Barbara? The kids?"

"Forget it."

After Dad and Steve moved in together later that same year, I put up a wall. I hated the situation for at least ten years and talked to Dad maybe three times. Mom's heart disease accelerated and my attention went to her. When she died and we had to let everyone know, I finally figured it took too much energy to hold in all that anger. Dad showed up at the services. He hugged me. We cried.

I began to visit him and Steve off and on after that. They got to know my wife, Barbara, and Dad was there when Trace was born. We felt something like a family again. In those rebuilding years, though, I still clutched to a tiny bit of rage— one last brick in my wall—for the new life Dad so easily took on. As I watch him slip away now, I can't help but feel that brick still there—the interminable heaviness of it—and wonder if Rob hasn't had the right idea all along.

Dad's still at the table looking out the window with the stupid shawl on and now he's crying. I drape the robe around him. I debate roughing him up, or maybe just toying with him. When exactly does it cross over into abuse?

"So, José stood you up again?"

"Yes. Second time this week," he says.

His eyes have caved in and his cheeks sag more these days. From the side, he reminds me of Grandma Vásquez, his mother, when she was on her way out. She always had this combination of worry and apprehension in her eyes, as though someone was going to burst in and scare her. I never noticed how wide her forehead was until I saw it in her open casket. Dad's forehead looks almost identical, but instead of the frizz job Hansen's Mortuary did with Grandma's hair, Dad's bald.

"Well, we'll have to just call him and see what the holdup is."

"Don't bother," Dad says. "He's a dog, anyway."

"What do you mean? A dog?"

Dad looks at me with the Grandma face, and for a second I think he knows me again.

"Who did you say you are?"

"I'm Earl. Dr. Earl. Are you feeling okay, Mr. Madrid? Or is it Mrs. Madrid?"

"I don't need a doctor."

"Dad, it's me. Your son."

"I don't have a son."

"You have two. Twins. Let's get up and get you to bed."

He shifts around in the chair and he leans forward, giving in. I lift him up, close his robe, and lead him down the hall. The place sparkles thanks to Marjorie, but every time I visit, something changes. Perfect rectangles of un-sun-bleached paint on blank walls mean he's taken another picture down. Books end up in the bathtub; plates go tucked under the couch cushions. I found a set of forks in his old cowboy boots. In his room, a suit's laid out on the bed.

"Is this what you meant to wear today?"

"That's for José."

"Here, sit down. Where were you two headed?"

"Mr. Steak."

Mr. Steak's been closed for decades. It's now a yoga studio.

I remember the suit from a picture where he and Steve were dressed up for some formal event. They matched.

"Let's put it away until tomorrow, okay?"

I hang the suit in his closet next to a row of dresses, closest to a maroon one. I slide the door shut, and his reflection in the mirrored panel stares back with the same pout. I want to push him, maybe slap him. I face him, feel that weight again, and tap the top of his shoulder instead.

There's an old yearbook open on his nightstand. Boys in white dinner jackets and black bow ties and girls with low black drapes from shoulder to shoulder, all of them with big hair, smile up at the ceiling. In the left margin, an autograph from a young man with a deep brow and slick hair says, "To Bird Dog: Don't ever change. Keep in touch. —José."

I slam the book shut.

Dad cries. "Why didn't he come?"

"I don't know. Maybe he doesn't love you anymore."

"What? Why?" Dad whimpers.

"We're going to have to take you somewhere soon, Dad. To a home."

"This is my home."

He looks around the room with the Grandma Vásquez face again, this time more lost. He pats around on the bed for something; looks back at me, eyes still damp. "Why did you stop loving me?"

I know the man we used to call Dad is in there. The man that ran behind us, training wheels off. Same guy that talked to us about sex and girls and using our heads. My shoulders tense and his eyes dart away from mine. I look where he looks

19

and see his reflection in the mirror again, and for just a second, I catch him. He hums the tune again.

"Stop, Mercedes. Please."

"Get out of here." He swats at me and I grab his wrist. I could break it with one twist. I lie his hand on his lap and turn toward his closet. I slide open the door and pull out the maroon dress and put it next to him.

"Here. We need to get you ready. For José."

"Is he coming?"

"Yes. He's going to meet us at Mr. Steak."

BLACK ANGUS IS the closest thing to what Mr. Steak was. Probably a little brighter and cleaner. The hostess takes us to a quiet corner—my request—and I shake my head each time a staffer passes by and gives me *the look*.

Our server, Manny, stutters on drink orders he's so distracted.

"He'll have a Coke," I say. "Water's fine for me."

I cut Dad's steak and feed him a few bites. He loves the mashed potatoes. Always has. For our sixteenth birthday, Mom and Dad dragged Rob and me to Mr. Steak. We really just wanted to be dropped off somewhere, like Pizza Hut or the mall, but they refused. When Rob's steak came out, he cut into it like he was killing it. He tipped his plate on accident and the filet fell in his lap. We laughed so hard that Mom threw up a little bit in her mouth.

After our dinner, Manny sets the Sky-High Mud Pie on the table and Dad looks right past it. He has forgotten he ordered it, the same way he forgot about José. Hasn't mentioned him once since we sat down. Maybe I'll take the dessert to go and put it in Dad's Frigidaire, where he'll find it the next day. Or not at all. I think today will be the last day he'll use his kitchen appliances.

He takes a sip of his soda on his own and leans back, resting his head on the high-backed, cushioned booth. He clasps his white-gloved hands over his protruding belly covered in satiny red fabric. He rests his eyes. I consider yanking off the matching pillbox hat tilting jauntily on his bald head. But I leave it. I'm the one who dressed him. It's best to keep him—and me—calm as long as possible. I'll never see him like this again. At a restaurant, on a date, dressed to kill.

TIFFIN AT DUCKWORTH'S

IN HER CRISP white oxford shirt and red apron, black hair pulled back tight into a high bun, Asia, the server, flaps closed her notepad.

"I'll be right out with drinks," she says. "And happy birthday, hon."

She winks at Archie, eleven years old today, but eleven years old yesterday, and the day before that. They'd only said it was his birthday to get a free dessert. That trick works everywhere.

"See?" Dad says.

"I think she winked because she's trying to proposition me," Archie says. "Did you see those bedroom eyes?"

"Archie!" Dad raises his finger at his youngest son.

"You don't even know what that means," Lars says.

Lars, Archie's recently-turned-fourteen-year-old brother, shakes his head. The three of them had gone to the Cheesecake Factory for Lars's special day, where Archie managed to make a server cry with his taunts about her teeth. He'd do well at one restaurant, not so well at others.

"Do too. It means when a girl wants to fu—"

"Zip it, Archie," Dad says.

"Yeah, Archie. Zip it," Lars says.

"Both of you, you hear me. This is Duckworth's. Don't act like asses."

"Dad said asses!" Archie snorts and bangs the table, clanging the silver service.

"Shhh!" Dad slaps his hand over Archie's.

A few tables away, another birthday celebration erupts with a small crew of Duckworth's servers marching and clapping, carrying over a lone sparkling candle stabbed into a chocolate cupcake. Their jazzy version of "Happy Birthday to You" increases in speed and rises in pitch. They're known for their singing ability at Duckworth's, not to mention their gourmet breads. The restaurant permanently smells of something baked, the scents of wheat competing with corn competing with rye.

"How long do we have to keep eating out?" Lars says. He taps the table, rolls his eyes.

"Until I learn how to cook," Dad says.

"You made that VDB the other morning." With a quick head toss, Archie clears some of his young Justin Bieber bangs from his forehead. He drops into a spot-on English accent. "Wouldn't you agree, dear brother, that the VDB father made was a most savory dish?"

"I'm going to get a set of clippers." Dad hits the table with resolve. "I'm going to get a set of clippers and I'm going to start cutting both of your hair myself. Crew cuts for both of you. That's what I got when I was your age. We didn't have a choice. Look at you, Archie. On track to have girl hair. And Lars, I can't keep buying that paste shit for that pomp of yours. Is that really in these days? You need to turn that hair down."

"No, Dad, I need that," Lars says.

"Yes, Father, he needs that paste shit," Archie says. "Now then, good chap, wouldn't you agree that the VDB Father made was most scrumptious?"

"Yes, it was good," Lars says. "Dad, please. I don't want a crew cut. Those are gay."

"What does he mean? VDB?" Dad says.

"Very delicious burrito," Lars says. "It's this new thing he's doing. TLAs."

"What?"

"Three-letter acronyms," Lars says.

"Father, why do you have that HWT in your dressing table drawer?" Archie taps the table.

"What? My what? Speak normal."

"You know, Father, that Hair With Tape on it." Archie pantomimes pulling a wig down on his own head.

Lars snorts, grabs his napkin to hide his wide braces-covered teeth.

"Shut. Up." Dad yanks Archie's wrist.

Asia arrives with sodas for Dad and Lars and a kettle of hot water with an assortment of teas for Archie. After studying the bags, he goes with English Breakfast. Asia sets down Duckworth's signature White Sweet Cornbread loaf for the table, and then claps twice to summon the ladder and honey. Another server rolls a six-rung ladder to the table, and another follows her with a ceramic jug of honey. The ladder-roller takes the jug, climbs up the ladder, and places it on the top step. She climbs down and flourishes her hand to grant Asia permission to proceed. Archie claps and wiggles in his seat.

Asia climbs to the top, secures herself in a leather strap around her waist, then takes the jug and hugs it in one arm. With her free hand, she plunges the honey dipper into the jug, then leans back on the ladder, raising her hand over her head, aiming the painfully slow drip of honey over the cornbread. This happens with every order of Duckworth's White Sweet Cornbread.

"Say when," she says.

Archie stops clapping and gazes up at Asia. He quits the proper English and falls into a smooth baritone voice. "Oooh, baby girl, you don't know what you're doing to me drizzling that honey all up on my sh——"

Dad whacks Archie on the back of the head.

Asia stops, drops the dripper back into the jug.

"Sir?" she says. Only the slight twinkle of holiday music fills the silence.

"What? What, punk ass?" Archie shoots up out of his chair. "You going to do me like Momma did?"

Asia steps down the ladder.

"Archie, sit." Dad pushes him back into his seat. "He's fine. He's fine," Dad assures Asia, who's looking at her Duckworth's fellow cast members for answers. They shrug and back away.

"We're fine," Dad says. "Right, guys? We're fine."

Lars nods and Asia turns away with the jug in the direction opposite her coworkers.

Dad leans in. "We are not to talk about your mother," he says through gritted teeth.

He digs a fork into the honeyed cornbread, shoves a mound of it onto his plate. He goes at it like he hasn't eaten in a while. He washes it down with a big gulp of soda, draining half the glass.

"What if we——I mean——what if I want to visit her?" Lars says.

"We'll talk about that later." Dad takes more cornbread. "Come on, guys. Dig in."

The boys' mother, Detective Gail Matthews of the Santa Ana Police Department, has been in custody for three weeks. She'll go up for trial soon, and the prosecutor wants to call in the boys as witnesses. Lars, yes. Archie, no way. He is still getting over some of the physical injuries.

Archie breathes and stares up. Pastel-painted scenes from classic children's literature—Jack climbing the beanstalk, Rapunzel letting her hair down, and the Big Bad Wolf knocking—cover the ceiling like the Sistine Chapel.

"I need to go to the bathroom," he says. "I don't feel so good."

"Lars, go with him," Dad says.

"I don't need to go."

"Go."

"But, Dad."

"Okay. Fine. Just go, Archie. By yourself. And no malarkey."

"No, Father, absolutely not," Archie says, British again. "I will not tarry."

"That's right, you won't," Dad says.

Archie stands, bows at his father and brother. He sticks his hand in the cornbread and scoops a chunk into his mouth. He runs off before Dad can say anything.

"I want my own room," Lars says. "I can't keep sharing with him."

"We'll work on that. I was thinking of turning the office into your bedroom."

Lars shakes his head. "She's not coming back, is she?"

"No. Not for a long time. It's best to forget her for a while. For Archie's sake."

"I guess it's true," Lars says.

"What's true?" Dad shovels more cornbread.

"That he's your favorite and I'm hers."

26

"God, no. That's not it at all."

"Then why did she beat the fuck out of Archie?" Lars says.

"Watch the goddamn language. And we are not to— listen to me, son. Your mom had a stressful job. How do I put this? Some people have a threshold, you know? Like a limit. Look: your brother's always been a little wisenheimer."

"It's gotten worse," Lars says.

"I know. That's what the psychologist expected. Son, listen. Hear me on this one. I've never had to worry about you. Ever since you were a baby, you just...complied. You're the easy one. Please, just keep being that way."

Dad scans the room. "Where is that damned kid?"

"See?" Lars shakes his head. "That's all you do. Worry about him."

"Didn't you hear what I just said? You're the calm in this swirling shit storm of ours.

You just turned fourteen and I need you to act like it. I need your help keeping this family together. Do you hear me? Now, please. Go check on your brother. God knows what he's up to."

"ARCHIE?" LARS PUSHES the restroom door open. In the light blue bathroom covered in pictures and cartoons of snips and snails and puppy dog tails, from one of the stalls, a voice strains. Under the door, Archie's boat-shoed feet dangle just above the tile floor.

Lars pounds the stall door. "Arch, is that you?"

"Yeah." More straining.

"What are you doing?"

27

"Making an MSP," Archie says.

"Mean Stinky Poop?" Lars says.

"Yeah."

"Dad wanted me to make sure you weren't messing around."

"Negative," Archie says.

"Well, hurry up." Lars checks his hair in the mirror. He'd love to show Mom his new style. Tell her about the good progress he's made in algebra. Tell her for sure that one day he wants to be a detective. Not a boring-ass businessman like Dad. She would ask him about girls, and he'd be shy at first; then he'd fess up about one or two of them. More recently it was Sarah, the sophomore. They had Spanish One together, and they had partnered up last week for conversación.

"I'll be out in a jiffy." Flush. Archie emerges from the stall, his mischievous smirk gone. "You all right?" Lars says.

"It's all this restaurant food."

"I know," Lars says. "It's never as good as you think."

"Our meals come?"

"Should be there by now," Lars says.

Archie washes up, heads for the door.

"Hey. Be good for Dad. Okay?" Lars says. "He loves you a lot."

"I know. I will. What are you doing?" Archie says.

"I need to make too."

Archie leaves and Lars goes to work fast, before anyone else comes in. He jimmies open the locked toilet paper holders with a paperclip in his pocket, takes the rolls, and plunges them in the toilets. Archie would never have the chance to learn what Lars learned a long time ago: how to handle Mom.

When are these stupid fancy restaurants going to learn to put in those automatic water faucets and jet hand dryers you see at airports? He yanks the quarter-sized drain catches and pushes a thick roll of paper towels into the drains.

Spigots running full blast, he runs into each stall one last time and flushes until the toilets begin to overflow. One last glance in the mirror, water gushing over the basins. He is going to miss her, for sure. But what she did was wrong. Wow, was it bad. Archie would be messed up forever, no doubt about it. The kid just might go his whole life afraid of women.

Dad was always going on about living pissing distance from all these theme parks and how you would think it would make your kids safer and happier. Really, he said, it was like being stuck on a ride with all those small singing faces staring at you, with the lap belt always low and tight. That's one thing Lars and Dad agree on: all that so-called happiness nearby only makes you sadder.

Lars opens the side pocket of his cargo shorts and fishes around. Feels the slippery latex and the firm, soda can-sized cylinder. It isn't that he needs any attention. He gets plenty from girls and some women. They love his hair. He sets the canister on the wet counter. *Do it now.* While Mom's away, and while Dad is fixed on Archie. As always. Mom said crooks are so stupid because they always get caught. One of the last new words she taught him was *recidivist.*

He pulls the pin and tosses the can into the puddles forming on the floor. Thick, gray, oily smoke blasts from the can, spewing up and out into the bathroom. He'd picked up the smoke grenade in some of Mom's police gear in the home office. Some stuff she'd left lying around before they apprehended her. She never even missed it.

Lars runs out of the smoky bathroom, his veins coursing with a pump of adrenaline he's never felt. Screw Dad and his

29

goddamned clippers. Guy doesn't even have enough hair of his own. *Always the good little boy, huh? Not now. Not forever.*

Lars takes the purple latex gloves off and shoves them in the empty pocket of his cargo shorts. He's hungry now for some of that cornbread and stinging for the soda he hasn't touched. Maybe Asia will be at the table again. Archie's right: she does have some bedroom eyes.

WORKING ON IT

SLOW DAYS LIKE this, I consider parking my van somewhere on Garnet Avenue to drum up business. It's a good idea, but then I'd have to walk back home. Or I could just stay in Pacific Beach all day with the van, but without Pablo, it's lonely. Plus, I can't work on my art. I just finished *Closed Tuesdays* this morning. It's an old wooden frame, the backdrop a combination of postcards we got from St. Croix, rum and beer labels, and fragments of Jimmy Buffet's book. In the center is a small pile of real sand I hoisted from Frederiksted Beach, and on top of that is a tiny pirate's chest I grabbed from a client's kid. This piece would fit right in at that art market, Pangaea, in PB. One day, I'll have my own booth there to sell my work. I'll call it Soul Kitchen.

Now I'm looking out the kitchen window waiting for inspiration and for the phone to ring. There's a new couple in the Rose Creek Apartments across the street. Zonies. I'd say from Tempe. They look educated. The man is white like me, and the wife or girlfriend is Indian. My wife, Tanya, always thinks it's strange that most of my exes look nothing like her. She doesn't realize that the picture-perfect California blonde girl is indeed exotic in her own right. I tell her all the time she's the perfect woman for me. And I'm the luckiest bastard alive because of her.

I eat lunch around two thirty. Chili and cornbread I made for dinner last night. My phone rings while I'm rummaging in the shed. 602 area code. Arizona.

"Hello? Is this D.B. Handyworks?" A woman's voice, pitched and almost British sounding, the slightest "v" where the "w" is in the name of my business—*Handyvorks*.

"Yes, yes it is. What can I help you with?"

"What are your rates and availability?" She's so formal and courteous.

"Seventy-five an hour. But it also depends on the job. I'm available right now."

"It's just a shower curtain rod and our TV. We want to mount them."

"Done. When's a good time for you?"

"Today, if possible," she says.

I hold my tongue. Instead of, *You're the hot new Indian woman on the other side of the cul-de-sac,* I say, "Works for me. Where are you located?"

"You're going to laugh," she says. "I'm on Figueroa. I saw your van across the street."

"Ha! That is me."

"So you're not busy now?" she says. "You can come over?"

"Absolutely. Are you in the apartments?"

"Ah, yes. Unit Six. Ground floor."

I know exactly which unit. "Be there in ten minutes, okay?"

"Okay, thank you," she says.

Turnover at these units is fast. I doubt renters here sign one-year leases. Standing outside it, I can see why. Chipping paint. Gaps at the bottom of doorways. And the windows. Terrible. Single-pane. If the other side of our duplex was open, I'd suggest this couple be our neighbors. They deserve better.

She opens the door, and what I'd been imagining from fifty feet away looks stunning up close. Dark hair pulled up in a messy bun, small round face, narrow arms and shoulders, then wide hips and a protruding belly. Nothing more beautiful than a woman expecting. I see one, then I start to see them everywhere, and I try not to get excited, but it's hard to contain it when they're brimming over like this. I'd say she's about six months along, though you'd hardly know it, she's so tiny. If Tanya ever changes her mind about having kids, she'll be a gorgeous pregnant woman.

"Hello." I grip my Bucket Boss in the woman's doorway, tools up and shining.

"That was quick." She smiles. Perfect teeth.

I thumb over the back of my shoulder, then offer my hand. "Dirk."

"Zareen." She pulls her hand away and a chocolate Lab barrels by her and pushes into my leg. His whole rear end shakes.

"Rama," she says. "Down."

"It's okay." I scratch him and he wiggles. The jingle of his tags reminds me of Pablo.

"He'll just lick you to death," she says.

"We just lost our dog about a month ago."

"Oh, I'm sorry," Zareen says.

I shrug. "Yeah, it's tough."

Then, finally, she says, "Come on in."

Their tiny living room is warmer than ours. A bit cleaner, too.

"We want it here." She holds up an invisible TV over the useless electric fireplace. She glances back over her shoulder

33

and a strand of her hair falls into her face. "There's the mount."

"I'm not sure that'll hold it. Might be too small." I crouch to lift the TV off the floor. These TVs today could practically float, and this will probably fit fine with the mount she's bought. I just want to stretch this job out.

"I can get a different one," she turns to me. Her bump in full view.

"I can do that for you. I'll include it in the job."

"Well, let me show you the shower," she says. "I bought the rod already."

She leads me down a short hallway off the bedroom. On a small table covered in a bright cloth is a shrine, and at its center, surrounded by candles and incense, sits a little pink-skinned elephant god with dreamy eyes. One more thing I can't stop staring at.

"Dirk?" Zareen calls from the bathroom.

"Sorry, I was just looking at the layout. I've never been inside one of these units."

"Here it is." She points to a box next to the shower.

"Tell you what. I'll do the shower rod right now, then go get the right mount. I can come back later or do that tomorrow. It'll take a bit longer. About an hour or so."

Rama nuzzles my free hand.

"Rama, come." Zareen goes to the living room, checking her phone.

"Can you finish the mount today? My husband really wants that done soon."

She moves around me, keeping Rama close.

"Can do," I say.

"And how much?" she says. "For everything?"

"Hundred bucks. No charge for sourcing the mount. That okay?"

She hesitates. I've seen this before. Women of the house get a little intimidated when given all that power with a man they don't know. Some just jump right in and say yes. And some let you stick around after the job's done to have a little fun while hubby's away. Used to, I should say. Some used to do that. No more. Never again.

"Yeah, that sounds good."

"Well, I've got all I need here," I head for the bathroom. "I'll just get started, okay?"

She seems to bow. Maybe that's why I like the exotic ones. They know how to respect men. She looks at the front door. I have to stop thinking like that. *Stop it, stop it, stop it.*

"Come, Rama," she says.

"So when's the baby due?"

She tries to hide her bump with her hands. "Oh, early May."

"Congratulations. Do you know what you're having?"

"No, not yet," she says. "We'll find out soon. Do you have children?"

"No. No we don't."

She smiles. "I need to make a couple of calls, so just let me know if you need anything. I'll be outside. Come, Rama."

Rama follows her and I go to work.

I pass the elephant. Not only do I want to take it, I want to break my promise and talk Zareen into one of those flings like back in the day. *Focus. Think of the art. The elephant.* How nice it would look. That's how the pure side of me works: a fully formed idea for a piece will just spill into my head and there it is, pulsing and eating at me until I can bring it to life.

I hate stealing from a client, but sometimes their things have a tiny voice saying, *Come on, take me. They'll never notice.* And I don't think six or seven times is a go-to-jail crime, not when it's fritter like a toy pirate chest or a doll's head. Besides, I need them for my real life's work. Handymanning is what helps pay the bills. Assemblage is what makes my heart tick and keeps me from wronging Tanya.

My ideal life is to have a studio to work on my craft. Tanya's a financial analyst at Goring Chemix, and says she likes being the breadwinner. She knows and I know that assemblage may never pay the bills, but maybe I could get so good at it that people will want to put my stuff in their homes and businesses, and then I've got a little career. Someday my art could be museum quality.

I'm back home, prepping dinner before I go back out. Tonight, it's roasted eggplant pitas, hummus, and a salad. Tanya just got in. She stays quiet when it's been a long day. Calls it her transition time.

"Wine?"

"Yes." She rubs her neck.

"I have to go back to work tonight," I say.

"Did you leave the glue gun running?" she smirks as I pour. Comments like that used to kill me early on. Now I just let them slide. Now that we know our places.

"No, I mean, *work* work. I have a job. Across the street."

"Oh? Who?" She sips.

"New couple. The wife called today. They need a shower curtain rod, which I already did, then I'm going to mount their flat screen."

"Tonight?"

"Yeah, it won't take long. They really wanted it all done today."

I serve her dinner. She leans over the plate and breathes it in.

"You're so good to me," she says. She takes my rough hand, places it on her chest.

"I should go, so I can finish it up and get home."

"You're not going to eat?" she dips into her hummus.

"I'm not hungry." I run my hands over her neck. She drops her head and accepts. "I'll give you a back rub tonight."

"Deal," she says. "Love you. See you in—how long?"

"Hour or so."

I take my bag and the new mount and walk across the cul-de-sac. The evening sky is Southern California pink.

Zareen answers and Rama charges.

"I have the right mount. Almost an even exchange." I set it down next to the TV. "Husband home?"

"Not yet. He's working late tonight," she says. Kitchen is steamy with spices. Smells like chicken tikka. One of my favorites.

"What's he do?"

"Biotech. Up in La Jolla."

"My wife's in biotech too."

She moves around quickly, putting things away in the kitchen.

For a second I think she might fix me a plate, offer some wine. *Stop it.*

"You don't mind if I leave for a little while?" she says.

"That's fine. If I finish early, can I lock up? You can pay me later. You know where I live." I smile, but she doesn't smile back. She pats Rama. I know when I've gone too far. I can read it all over their faces.

She grabs her phone off the kitchen counter. Scrolls. "Oh, look. He'll be home sooner. He'll be back while I'm out."

"That works, too."

"Do you want me to lock Rama in the bedroom?" she says.

"No, he's good here. Aren't you, buddy?" Rama can't get enough scratches and I don't mind giving them.

"Okay, well, thanks, Dirk. I'll see you later."

"Okay, sounds good." I give her a thumbs up.

She leaves and, before I get to work, I pop up to make sure she's really gone. Car's out of the driveway. Job's going to take only thirty minutes.

The kitchen is stocked with organic food and great snacks. They buy the good whole milk and Vitaminwater, and they have a delicious gouda cheese. I'll have to find that one. I lift the lid off what she was cooking—definitely tikka. I stop myself from sticking a spoon in to try some.

Rama follows me into the living room. Their DVDs are mostly romcoms and yoga. In their bedroom, their closet resembles a J. Crew. He's a tighty-whitey man and hers are full coverage, some black, some white, mostly tan. Down at the bottom she's got a couple stringy things. Pink. Red. The second bedroom is filled with baby stuff. I could build it all for them. I'd be happy to do that.

I get to work, moving fast with Buffet jamming in my ear buds. *Focus. Change your state. Power move.* I don't want to go back in their bedroom, and I don't want to see the elephant.

38

What if Rama has a camera in his collar? The way he follows me around, I wouldn't be surprised if Zareen busts back in and kicks me out for opening her panty drawer.

TV's up. I connect the cable cord, give it a test run. All systems go. I clench my fists as hard as I can. *Do not go back into their room. Do not touch the elephant.* I need to leave and go right across the cul-de-sac. Tanya's there, waiting for me. The only person in the world who gets me and who's helped me. She paid for my counselors, sent me to Tony Robbins. I mean, she's the real saint here. I'll do anything for her. *Help me, Tanya. Help me right now.*

Then that fucking little voice. The *they'll-never-even-miss-it* voice. But yes, they will miss it. A lovely, rosy god like that, no matter how small, will be felt. These people keep track. I know it. Guy probably counts his ties.

It's so beautiful though. I've been working on the finished piece in mind. It'll be dedicated to Tanya, as all my pieces are. Me making for her what she'll probably never make for me. My brainchildren.

The elephant god fits nicely inside my Bucket Boss, nestled in with my worn tools. It's going to look perfect in that glass case I found at the Salvation Army. I'm going to adorn it with tiny blue flowers from our wedding decorations and install a yellow light underneath.

Should I leave a note for them? Maybe just my business card with the amount on the back. I take checks. Card. Cash.

Headlights pour into their front window. I catch a glimpse of our place across the way and wish I could teleport over there. A car door slams. A tall man unbends himself from his coupe. Husband is home. He opens the front door.

"Dirk?" he says.

"Hi, yes. I was just leaving. Did you want to take a look?"

"I'm Ben," he offers his hand. "Thanks for doing all this today. It looks great."

"You got it." They're such good people. You can tell it in the way they look and smell.

"I forgot one thing," I tell Ben. "A tool. In the bathroom."

"Sure." He sets a reusable grocery sack down, grabs the TV remote.

I face the empty altar and put the god back. *Thank you, Lord.*

In the living room, Ben stops channel surfing. "Hundred, right?"

"Seventy-five."

"You sure?" he says.

"I'm sure. Neighbor discount."

BACK HOME, THE shower runs. I open the bathroom door and Tanya shuts off the water. She steps out, grabs her towel. She's a stunning nude. Makes me wish I painted instead of gluing shit together. I'd love to have her model for me all day. She combs out her long blonde hair with smooth strokes, then reaches for her toothbrush. She knows I'm watching, so she moves slower. I start to undress as she wraps her towel up over herself. She rinses her mouth and dabs her lips.

"Can I still take you up on that back rub?" she says.

"Yeah. Let me take a shower first."

She picks up my dirty clothes and winks.

I notice something. The space behind the vanity spigot is bare. No pills. She keeps them there so she doesn't forget to take one each morning. The foil pack shines from the trash bucket. There are only a few empty blisters. The rest are filled with her month's supply. *Oh my God. Is she going off them?*

I get in the shower. Water's still warm but turning cool.

Around the time we lost Pablo and cried for a couple of days, Tanya said I'd been a great stay-at-home dad for him, and that she could see me doing it for real kids. We always said he was like our child, and joked that if we didn't have him, we might have four kids by now. That's my other ideal life: father to Tanya's children. Maybe she's starting to see it too.

The water goes cold, and I stay under the stream until I get used to it. It doesn't take long. You figure out quickly how your body prefers the shock. How much better you feel when you go against what feels good. It's like listening to the other little voice, not the bad one, and actually doing what it tells you.

MY FIRST WAR

GILBERT FERNANDEZ KNEW it was well past midnight. He'd heard they take you in the wee hours, that if you weren't standing at attention as instructed—say, you had decided to lie down and fall asleep—they'd beat the crap out of you. He shivered despite the various layers of the Warrior Scout Cadet issue uniform: the weather-proof jacket and camo pants, the constricting bodysuit underneath with the wire node at the chest. He figured he was near Norco with the strong smell of cattle fields in the air. The blindfold wouldn't come off either. It was adhered, like a second skin. Blinking was impossible.

When his parents had dropped him off hours before, they said nothing, just opened his door, walked him ahead a few paces, and left. His mom had whispered *Happy Birthday* in his ear before they left the house. She had been teary in the days leading up to his departure, saying over and over how she couldn't believe her little boy was turning sixteen. How he was almost a man.

Gilbert slid a boot-covered foot ahead, praying he wasn't on the edge of a cliff. He reached out in all directions and felt nothing. He kept thinking of Mya, his girlfriend, how that morning after English, she had pulled him into one of the unisex bathrooms in the Language Arts building and locked the door. She knelt in front of the toilet, held her braids back, and threw up. He handed her some toilet paper, patted her back. They'd been denying the positive test she had shown him weeks before.

"We need to figure this out," she had said.

Whatever they chose would be lifelong: guilt or responsibility.

"We'll talk about it when I get back from Rubicon," he said.

"I can't keep waiting," she said. "It's my body."

A boy's voice in the distance called out. "Hello? Anyone there?"

Gil shouted back. "Hey."

More boys yelled out.

"*Hello?*"

"*Where are you?*"

"*Over here.*"

An air horn blared, then a man's voice, deep and raspy, boomed over them.

"Find your brother. Now! Three to a team."

Gilbert darted ahead, arms reaching in front of him. He slammed into someone, grabbed hold, feeling arms, shoulders, a neck. Another body ran into them, hands gripping and tugging. They patted each other, panting urgently in the chilly air. One of them was on the verge of tears. Someone else rammed into their triad.

"We're full," one of the three said, clutching Gil's jacket.

A deep breathing, steady and calm, the voice quiet and intense, spoke into Gilbert's ear.

"Name your team." This wasn't either of his newfound teammates.

"Guys, what's our name?" Gil said.

"The Ninja Assassins," one said.

"Fuck no," the other one said. "We're Balls Deep."

"What's that?" Ninja Assassins said.

"Sex. Something you two bitches ain't getting."

"You don't know that," Gil said.

"So, is it settled?" Balls Deep said.

"Whatever," Gil said. "I don't care."

A deep laugh erupted in Gil's ear. "Hey, they named themselves Balls Deep."

More laughter broke out around them. The voice spoke in Gil's ear again, while a blunt object was thrust into his side.

"You better start caring," it said.

At the required Rubicon Orientation Meeting last month, an out-of-shape Warrior Scout named Jeff, who smiled a lot and whose left shoulder rose up every so often, went on about war not being what it used to be. How our enemies now hack our computing systems, or poison us from afar, like cowards. American boys don't know how to fight anymore, he said. Our culture *needs* warriors.

After the presentation, the parents at the meeting scrolled through pages of liability release forms, clicking their approval. And then, Jeff sent them away. He locked the door, sealing the boys—about ten in Gil's session—inside the defunct Hallmark card shop at the Dos Lagos Mall. Jeff dimmed the lights and stood in front of the boys. He scowled, his shoulder locked in place.

"What's the loneliest number?" he asked as he paced.

"One?" Gilbert had said.

"Zero." Jeff stopped, stared him down. "Do you know what zero is? Zero is a quitter. Someone who gives up. Someone who fucks his brother."

Jeff paced again. "I'm going to tell you a little story. 'Bout a guy that came to Rubicon and decided he was going to go AWOL. Absent Without Official Leave. Do you know what

44

happened to him? He was electrocuted and died. Don't be the Zero. Don't fuck your brother."

Here in the dark, the owner of the voice pushed Gilbert ahead. Still clutching each other, Balls Deep moved forward, boots scraping the dirt, six feet tripping over each other.

"Wait here." The man stopped them.

More feet shuffling, boys murmuring, some shuddering. A van door sliding up.

The airhorn again, and another voice, this one meaner.

"Get in, lie down, and shut up. This will be your last, and I repeat last, opportunity for sleep. You're going to need it."

Balls Deep scrambled inside and fell onto a pile of squirming bodies. Elbows hitting blindfolds, boots grazing mouths, their groans and whimpers muffled. The van door slid down, and Gil thought of Mya again, that time she had come with him and his friends out to the desert to ride dirt bikes. She watched and waited, said her dad would kill her if she got on one of those things. On one of the rounds, Gilbert stayed back with Mya. They rolled down the door of the box truck, and then took off their clothes. If they couldn't agree on what to do soon, she was going to take care of it herself. They were already at eight weeks.

A SPRAY OF wetness hit Gil's forehead and nose, followed by a tug at his temple. A hand ripped off his blindfold, like the sting of duct tape tearing out your arm hair. Gilbert blinked and rubbed his eyes, shielding them from the blinding sun. Morning had come.

Balls Deep and the other trios of boys stood shoulder to shoulder in a large semi-circle in the middle of an open desert.

The ground was cracked like misshaped tiles under their feet, no plants in any direction. Only a ridge of low mountains felt like protection with the sun and sky domed over them. The landscape was familiar to Gilbert. He knew this kind of land was sometimes called a playa, the beach of an old lake bed, but with no water. They were the best places to pin the throttle on a bike and leave a single trail of dust behind you for miles. A Warrior Scout with a severe crew-cut sprayed the other two boys flanking Gilbert. He got his first look at his team: one a short and thick Asian boy, the other a skinny white guy with choppy blond hair.

A tall Warrior Scout stood at the center of the circle and shouted, "Atten-hut!"

The boys straightened up. A smile spread across his face. "Good morning, girls," he said, "Welcome to Hell."

In unison, other Warrior Scouts standing in front of each group of three stepped forward and dropped logs at the trios' feet.

"This is your Fourth Man," the Sergeant said. "Take it with you."

The Scouts tossed a placard at the boys' feet, along with a canteen and a brown packet.

"Follow the map," the Sergeant said.

Gilbert picked up the items. The packet was a raisin nut mix. He handed it to the Asian boy.

"Sir?" The Asian boy raised his hand to the Scout in front of Balls Deep. "I have a peanut allergy."

"Tough titties," the Scout said.

"Pick up your man and move out. Now," the Sergeant said.

46

"IT'S ABOUT TO be noon." The blond boy pointed at the sun, marching ahead of Gilbert and the Asian boy. "Been walking at least three hours." Gilbert carried the Fourth Man on his shoulder, the Asian boy keeping up alongside him. Gilbert had been running over how he was going to tell the Bowlings, Mya's parents. Especially her father. Gilbert figured Mya could enroll in the teen mom classes at Santiago High. She'd have to quit volleyball. He'd quit football so he could lifeguard through the school year to save money. They'd graduate and move in together. Go to college. Raise a family. They could make it work.

"Where do you think we are?" the Asian boy said.

"I'm Gilbert. Who are you?"

"Mexico," the blond boy shouted back.

"How do you know?" Gilbert walked faster to catch up to him.

"Jayden," the Asian boy said. "My name's Jayden Kalyanapong."

The white boy stopped, turned around. "Did you say Jayden?"

"Yeah."

"Fucking shit. That's my name, too," the blond boy said.

"So how do you know we're in Mexico?" Gilbert said.

"I heard a couple of those douchebag Scouts say they were going to run into Mexicali for something."

"So, we're breaking the law?" Asian Jayden said.

"That's all you do is ask questions, isn't it, chink?" Jayden said.

"I'm not Chinese, you asshole," Asian Jayden said. "I'm Thai."

47

"Oh, so that's why you're so pretty."

"Enough," Gil said. "Here, take this."

He rolled the Fourth Man off his shoulder and shoved it onto white Jayden.

"Yo, I told you, man, my rotator's all fucked up."

"Come on," Gilbert said. "I know what a rotator injury is, and you're fine."

He studied the card, scanned the dusty wasteland. They'd drifted apart from the other teams still marching forward. Far off in the opposite direction, shimmering on the horizon, Gilbert thought he saw the low skyline of a city, the air above it brownish against the blue. In those raw moments when Mya both cursed and cried with joy, when Gilbert had stayed by her side, the two of them wallowing in fear, she had said something about Rubicon being a big mind game. Her father had been a Lieutenant in the Warrior Scout Association, had given recruitment talks at one time. He must have let something slip in front of Mya.

"You ever hear of guys quitting this thing?" Gilbert said.

"Going AWOL? Fuck no. What? Are you thinking about that?" White Jayden said.

"I've got a lot going on right now," Gilbert said. "With my girlfriend."

"Me, too. My girl's been acting crazy and shit. Let's just keep moving," white Jayden said.

"Same here," Asian Jayden said. "My girlfriend be all like, 'What's up with you, boy?'"

"Shut up. You don't have a girlfriend," White Jayden said.

"Neither do you," Asian Jayden said.

"How do you know?"

"My girlfriend's pregnant," Gilbert said. "I need to go. I need to be with her."

Gilbert turned the other direction and started walking. If that was Mexicali, Calexico was on the other side, and Interstate 8 was only a few miles from that. He could hitchhike to San Diego, catch a train back to Corona.

White Jayden ran up to Gilbert. "What the hell are you doing?"

"Going AWOL," Gilbert said. It was possible that Mya might be taking care of it on her own right now. He could see why she wouldn't want to wait. She'd had her whole year planned out. As a junior, she already had three schools looking at her for volleyball. She wanted to be an anesthesiologist. She was still mad at herself, she had kept saying, for being so irresponsible. It had hit Gilbert just as hard. He knew he was equal parts in the wrong.

"No," Asian Jayden said. "You'll die."

"You can't leave," White Jayden said. "You can't just quit."

"I'm not. I'm doing what they want. I'm being a man."

"If you leave, I'll fucking kill you," White Jayden dropped the log at their feet.

"Come at me, bro," Gilbert said.

"Guys, no. Come on, let's just go." Asian Jayden pointed toward the other boys.

When they could steal a few minutes between classes or their practices, and when she wasn't queasy, little snaps of the future popped around them, Mya talking about how cute it would be if they kept it. A beautiful blend of her black and his brown skin, wavy hair, maybe his light eyes. Gilbert imagined this, too, and thought a lot about the day-to-day—how he'd

49

seen his cousins who'd started families early, and though they complained about all the stuff you have to buy and bring with you, and how you're up all night, the hard parts went by pretty fast.

Behind them, dust billowed up, the brown clouds moving fast in their direction. A dark utility vehicle emerged, covered in dirt. It pulled beside them and the passenger window rolled down.

"Atten-hut," a Warrior Scout said.

Balls Deep came to attention, Gilbert a few beats behind the Jaydens.

"You're falling behind." The Warrior Scout pointed ahead. "What's the problem?"

"We're hungry," Asian Jayden said.

"Wah, wah, wah," the Scout said. "I said, what is the problem?"

"Sir, he wants to quit. He's going AWOL. He's quitting on us, sir." White Jayden had puffed up his chest.

"Pick up your Fourth Man." The Scout pointed at white Jayden.

White Jayden picked it up and stood tall.

"Now drop it."

"Sir?"

"Drop it."

Jayden complied.

"Pick it up," the Scout said. "Now drop it. Pick it up. Drop it. Keep going. Faster."

Jayden followed orders, huffing and starting to sweat.

"You know what's worse than a quitter?" the Scout said.

"Sir, no Sir," Gilbert and Asian Jayden said.

"A snitch." The Scout cocked his head at the driver. "Buzz him."

White Jayden, about to pick up the Fourth Man, convulsed. The body suits and that node at the chest. Electrocution was a real thing. Gilbert thought it was a joke. Jayden hit the ground twisting into a fetal position, his twitching body stirring up the dirt.

"Something you want to tell me? Fernandez, is it? Or are you going to spill the beans, Kalyana-whatever-the-fuck? Someone better start talking, or I'll fry your little pal here."

White Jayden writhed, his face contorted.

"I was going to leave, sir," Gilbert said.

"Go on." The Scout let up on the shock. Jayden stopped wiggling.

"My girlfriend back home. She's pregnant, and I was, we were going to—"

"Stop. We know. Lieutenant Bowling's daughter. You're a royal fuck-up, you know that? He called this morning. Said to find you. Tell you it's been taken care of."

In between sleep and the absence of it, Gilbert had come up with some names. Gavin Mack if a boy, Cedella Teresa if a girl. For his mom. He'd kicked himself for doing something like that, such a girlish thing. He'd never quit anything. He'd always played to the end. In football, in class, at work, in those video games when he was kid. *My First War* was his favorite.

"You gonna cry, Cadet?" The Scout said. "Pick up that piece of shit and your Fourth Man and keep moving."

White Jayden, settled now, blinked up at Gilbert, squinting in the sun. He pressed his index finger into the Warrior Scout eagle emblem on his chest.

The node had irritated Gilbert since he dressed the night before. He had dropped his hand into the suit, his fingers meeting the tiny node. They were instructed to never tamper with their base layer.

White Jayden mouthed the word, "Run."

"I said get moving." The Scout pointed ahead.

Gilbert pulled off his jacket, then grabbed at his collar. The fabric held tight, and he couldn't untuck it, the one-piece pulling at his groin on each upward yank. With all the rage he'd been taught to bottle, with the hurt he'd just been delivered, Gilbert tore the fabric apart, the warm desert air hitting his bare chest. Maybe she hadn't done it. It was all a mind screw, right?

The Warrior Scout jumped out of the truck. He reached for Gilbert. Asian Jayden pushed the Scout as he walked by, and White Jayden jumped to his feet. The driver pressed something from where he sat, and both boys seized and fell to the dirt squirming.

Gilbert turned into a sprint. He didn't look back to see the Warrior Scout who, after Gilbert had taken a sizable lead on him, had stopped chasing him, and was screaming into his radio.

The flickering skyline wasn't a mirage, and Gilbert kept running toward it, dehydrated and hungry, but revived like he was super-powered, as though he had found an extra reserve of strength, or a 1-Up.

In Mexicali that evening, he found a pay phone outside an OXXO. He didn't know how to use it, so he asked a man walking into the convenience in his best Spanish if he could borrow his cell phone. The man handed it to him. Mya's number was the only one, besides his parents' and his own, that he had memorized by heart. She answered on the third ring.

"Hey," he said. "It's me."

"What are you doing? You're supposed to be at—"

"Did you do it? Did you go to the clinic? I wanted us to wait."

"No," she said. "But I told my parents. I couldn't hide it. You're pretty much going to die out there."

"Why?"

"My dad knows all those guys. They're going to mess you up."

"They'll have to find me," Gilbert said. "I quit."

The Mexican man circled his hand at Gilbert. "*No más. Ándale.*"

"I have to go. Please don't do anything until I get back. I have a plan. Bye."

He tossed the phone back to the man. "*Gracias. ¿Tienes cinco dolares? Tengo hambre.*"

The man shook his head, but fished out his wallet, taking out an American five.

"*¿Eres uno de esos niños soldados, no?*"

"Yeah," Gil said. "Sí. Child soldier."

"*¿Escapado?*"

"Yeah." Gil pocketed the five and smiled.

The Mexican man shook his head and laughed, pulling the OXXO door open.

Across the street, a taqueria twinkled with red and green lights, the menu said al pastor, vampiros, suizas. They had jamaica and horchata. Gilbert gripped the bill in his pocket and walked ahead, not looking back.

DAUGHTERS

MAIDEN VOYAGE

DOT'S THUMBS HOVERED over her phone screen, waiting for Mom's reply.

Mom: *Papa get there? How's his RV? Bigger than your father's shoebox?*

Dot fired back. *LOL Yes he's here thinks I'm 9 the way he hugs and kisses me*

Dad set out mismatched mugs of hot cocoa and a plate of donuts on the coffee table. Dot, next to Papa on the couch, glanced up at her father, shook her head no, then dove back into her phone. She scrolled through her apps, waiting for something new. Zoe texted. Then Rick, the guy Dot had been talking to.

Zoe: *so bored I hate summer already how's even more boring Oregon? let's get a sack when you get back hey that rhymes* ☺

"It's swimsuit season," Dad said to Papa. They reached for their mugs and donuts.

"Dad." Dot glared at him, then went back to texting Zoe. Dot needed Rick advice.

"Dorotea." Papa patted her knee. "*Mira*. I want to show you something."

He opened his leather folio to his graph papers. The family tree. Again.

"Can you put that down for a minute." Dad pointed at her phone.

Dot rolled her eyes, set it on the coffee table.

"I've been going to the Idaho State Archives." Grandpa flipped through the pages. "The archives have the best records. Did you know we're Spaniards? Not *Vascos* like I thought all this time. I think this is my great-grandfather. Geraldo Saturnino Betancourt de Hernandez. It says he was born in Valencia, Spain."

"This is great, Papa." Her phone buzzed and she grabbed it. Reply from Zoe. "I have to check something, okay?"

"Okay, *mi amor*, I'll wait for you." Papa winked.

Dad eyed her and she turned away from him, held up her phone and motioned to go outside. It was the only private place at Dad's tiny house. He shrugged and dipped his donut in the cocoa.

Once on the small porch, the blue glow of her phone soothed her. It was warm outside. She read his text again.

Rick: *Hey. Thinking of you. When do you get back to SEA? Meet up?*

Before she left Seattle, Dot had visited him at Starbucks and saw a couple of his chest hairs curl out of the top of his work polo shirt. Stuff like that used to gross her out, but this last time, it kind of wrecked her inside, just for a second. She'd call him next.

Zoe picked up on the first ring.

"I'm going to murder Bethany," Zoe said. "You know what the little shit did? She showed my mom my birth control. I'm like so totally fucked. I mean, my mom knew, but she like, didn't really know, you know? What are you doing? Did you call Rick? Don't call him yet."

"Wait like ten minutes, right?" Dot said, slowly pacing.

There was a light on in the little bedroom in Papa's R.V. Maybe he'd left it on. Dot stepped up the first step. The door was unlocked.

"Hells yeah. Longer if you want. But keep it short when you call him. Tease him. Say like, 'it's sooo hot here, is it hot there?'"

Dot pushed the R.V. door open. Except for the evening light coming through the windows, it was dark in the camper. The bedroom door was closed, as it was earlier when he gave her the five-second tour. The piney scent of Papa's aftershave—the smell he'd always had—covered up the more powerful odor of old man. Something like dirty laundry. There was a pile of hers and Dad's that needed washing. *Why would anyone live in a house without a washer and dryer?*

She made an even smaller lap in the kitchen/dining/living room space. "He wants to meet up when I get back."

"Do it," Zoe said. "But not at Starbucks. Go to like a park. Right before dark. Bring him something. No. Wait. Too soon. Put your hair up the way you did when you first met."

"How do you know all this stuff?" Dot stood in front of Papa's bedroom door. Mom always said to knock, never just walk into someone's bedroom. *But wait, no one's in there.*

"I don't know," Zoe said. "I'm *experienced.*"

"Well, yeah, I mean..." Dot laughed, gripped the doorknob, and turned. "You are on the pill, so..."

"Girl, you're about to be poppin' em too, getting you some man bun in a minute."

57

"He doesn't have a man bun. It's more like a ponytail thingy." Dot pushed the door open. Warm amber light spilled out. On the R.V. tours she took with Dad before he settled on building his own tiny house, she couldn't imagine him really living in one, and she let him know it. His response: quit channeling your mother. *What did that even mean?*

"It's definitely a man bun," Zoe said. "It's cute on him. He can pull it off."

The covers were lumped up to one side of the square mattress, and what she thought were the pillows, created a distinct mound in the center of the bed. *Typical man to not make the*—but there, extended out from the raised lumps, was the curve of a woman's calf, the white-pinkness of skin unmistakable. Dot scrambled backward and slammed the door shut.

"Oh my God!" she said into the phone.

"What?" Zoe paused. "Hold on. Bethany, get the fuck out of my room, I said. Wait. I gotta go. Call me later. You okay?"

"Yes. No. Bye." Dot hung up and ran out of the R.V. At Dad's porch, she couldn't look back. What if they—*she*—saw Dot and followed her?

Back inside, Papa patted the empty space next to her.

"Everything okay?" Dad said.

"Ven acá." Papa pointed at the pages. "This is you. And this is your father and mother. And this is me and your *abuelita*—*dios bendiga*—and these are my parents. Candelaria and Ignacio Betancourt. Your great-grandparents."

She avoided his eyes, clutched her phone.

"Sit down, honey." Dad said.

"I'm actually not feeling good." She held her stomach.

58

"Do you need some Pepto?" Papa said. "I have Pepto."

"What's wrong?" Dad said. "Who were you talking to? Was that that Zoe girl?"

"I need to go to bed," she said.

"We just started visiting," Grandpa said.

She still couldn't look at him.

"Dad, I need to go to bed." She pointed up to the loft.

"Okay. Whatever." He pushed his chair back and brought the ladder to the balcony. Dot climbed up without looking back. "Goodnight," she said.

Dad and Papa moved around quietly downstairs, putting things away, not saying much. *I'll see you tomorrows. Goodnights.* The front door opened, then shut.

From the loft window, Dot watched as Papa went back into his R.V. The rear end where his bedroom was faced away from her window, thank God.

She hid herself under the covers, fully clothed. She woke her phone and was about to text Mom. Maybe it was time to go back home. But wait, why did it scare her so much? Wouldn't Papa just introduce her?

"Honey? Are you okay?" Dad called up to her.

She couldn't answer him. Her eyes burned.

"Dottie?" The ladder creaked.

She shivered as though she were cold.

Dad's head and shoulders came into view. "What's wrong? Are you sick? Talk to me."

Dot turned in the bed and pushed herself up. She pulled her hair back and wiped her eyes.

"Daddy," she said, "Papa has someone in his camper. A woman."

He looked down, rubbed his brow. He never flinched like that. "Why don't you come down for a minute? Let's talk."

DOT: *NEED TO talk tomorrow*

Mom: *Sure. Everything okay?*

Dot: *Weirded out*

Mom: *Talk now?*

Dot: *No, it's late don't want to go outside*

Mom: *Tell me what's wrong*

Dot: *Papa has a doll*

Mom: *What? Like a toy??? A puppet? Explain, please*

Dot: *No it's a life-like woman.*

Mom: *I'll come for you tomorrow*

Dot: *Dad explained it Papa's lonely*

Mom: *Have you seen it? It's not a blow-up thing, is it? Where does he keep it?*

Dot: *Blow up?? It's in his bedroom in his RV I saw its leg when I was in there*

Mom: *What were you doing in there?*

Dot: *Nothing I was in there and just opened the door*

Mom: *I don't like the sound of any of this. I'm calling your father*

Dot: *No I'll handle it*

Mom: *What do you mean?*

Dot: *I'll be fine*

THE SUN WOKE her, and just as fast, the memories of last night's talk with Dad flooded in. Ramona was Papa's companion—just someone to keep him company on the road. Plus, men have *certain needs*.

Dot had stopped Dad's explanation right there the night before, when the terrible vision solidified in her head: her Papa, doing things with it based on what she'd only pieced together from Health & Wellness I and II, and from what Zoe had told her about how it felt. Dot herself had only been on her first date last Halloween with gross Evan Geller. They had held hands in the movies, kissed with a little bit of tongue, then he moved her hand up his own thigh, her palm grazing the stiffness in his Batman costume. She had wanted to leave right then. Zoe had told her that's just the beginning, girl.

Dad was shuffling around downstairs, getting food ready to take over to Grandpa's R.V. That was the new plan. Papa was going to *introduce* her.

What would Zoe do? Dot grabbed her phone to text her, but found it dead. A small rage stirred inside her for leaving the charger downstairs overnight. She put on her workout clothes and climbed down.

"Morning," Dad said. "Sleep okay?"

Dot plugged in her phone. "Yeah, fine."

"You still okay going over to Papa's?" he said. "It's probably better to just get that out of the way, I thought."

"Yeah, let's do it." Dot put on her running shoes. "It's probably better to just get the hell out of here," she whispered to herself. *That's what Zoe would do.*

Dot's phone came to life. Five texts, two likes, three Snaps, and a voice mail.

"Ready when you are," Dad said.

She left it charging, and on the way out, she eyed the keys to Dad's truck on the hook by the door. They'd gone for their second practice drive that week just yesterday, to the coast and back. She was almost ready for her maiden voyage—her first solo drive, Dad said. Once she was out on the road and her phone had more juice, she'd check her messages.

Dot stepped out into the warm air, and a memory struck her out of nowhere: years ago, right before Grandma's funeral began, when her casket was still open at the front of the church, Papa had leaned in and kissed his wife on the lips for the very last time. It had shocked Dot to see him kiss Grandma's corpse, but it was somehow the sweetest thing ever.

After breakfast, Papa cleared the plates and rinsed them in the tiny sink. *What if Dad gets a doll too? Both of them, hooking up with their latex—oh, God. Is that why Dad hasn't been dating? I mean, Mom's already got a boyfriend.*

"Did you have enough to eat?" Papa's face softened in a strange way.

Dot studied Ramona, opposite her in the dining booth. Ramona's eyelids were shut halfway and reminded Dot of old pictures of Marilyn Monroe. Zoe had explained that Marilyn looked like that because she was always blasted out of her gourd on painkillers. We'll try those one of these days, Zoe had said.

"What do you two, like, talk about?" Dot said.

"Honey, it's not like that." Dad placed his hand over Dot's. She quickly pulled away.

"Well, when I was little and had dolls, I talked to—"

She stopped herself. Papa shrunk, averted his eyes.

"I don't *play* with her like a baby doll," he said. "Ramona will never replace your *abuela*."

"Well, can I be her friend?" Dot said.

BFF Zoe, far away in Seattle, came right through Dot now, her raspy voice and that little lift at the end of her sentences. She was a master at getting what she wanted. In Intro to Drama last year in eighth grade, Zoe was the only one who was able to cry on cue.

"No," Dad said. "You tell Papa you're sorry right now."

"Dad, I'm serious. I just want to get to know her." Dot tilted her head, tapped Dad's hand. This was what he meant by channeling.

She reached for Ramona and touched her face. "So soft," Dot said.

"She's not bad," Papa smiled. "Right?"

"No, not at all." Dot said. "She's so—perfect."

According to Zoe, you could tell someone one thing, and be thinking something else.

"I'm glad, *mi híja*, I just didn't want you to be—scared."

Dot turned to Dad. "Do you think I could take her out for a ride? Just like around here, on the dirt roads and stuff."

"I don't think that's a good idea. No." Dad shook his head.

"Dad's been teaching me." Dot smiled at Papa.

"Absolutely not," Dad said.

"Just let her," Papa said. "I trust you, *mi cariña*."

"It'll be better—safer—to have someone in the car with me anyway." Dot stood, her smile for the both of them the most artificial she'd ever mustered.

DOT FLOORED THE gas in Dad's truck on the Interstate 84 ramp, thrusting them into a fast stream of traffic. Putting the pedal down hard stoked those little fires she'd been feeling inside lately. As though this awkward phase from girl to woman wasn't too bad after all—that you could harness it and go as fast as you wanted. She'd only been on the highway once and loved it. Back in Seattle, Dot had hardly sat in the driver's seat of Mom's Lexus, let alone blasted down the interstate. Seattle was a spaghetti bowl—Mom's words—of on ramps and exits, dropping in on them would take lots of skill. Out here, the drive was easy.

Dot rolled down the windows and sped up. The rush of air swirled their hair up above their ears. They'd go to the mall first, and then Dot could go finally into Victoria's Secret, alone.

"This is living, girl!" she yelled, and hit Ramona's arm for agreement. "Should I call you Grandma?"

Ramona stared ahead the way she had in Papa's R.V. She didn't look amused. Her brown hair had begun to tangle up from the air rushing in.

Cars zipped past them, and a punch of guilt shorted Dot's Zoe-like cackle. Paranoia began to seep in, like when she and Zoe and their friends smoked weed, someone—usually Dot—would say something about school or their parents, and crash the whole thing down. Zoe always made her feel bad about being the buzzkill. Dot checked her phone, but the voice from the Driver's Ed videos played in her ear: *One second of distracted driving can mean a lifetime of pain. Or even worse, death.*

MOM lit up on Dot's phone screen. Dad had already called three times. It had only been forty-five minutes at the most. Aren't all kids supposed to run away at some point? Mom did. Ran off with Dad when they were 19 because Mom's parents didn't approve of Dad. Dot loved that story. It was why things were always a little tense around Grandma and Grandpa Phillips when Mom and Dad were married. Like you had to be careful about everything.

Grandpa Betancourt? You could do whatever you wanted. He never made you feel bad. And neither did Dad, really. His only thing was trying to remind Dot who her friends were. Mom liked that Dot had friends like Zoe. She said the right people can have a good influence on you. Mom's friends were so cool. And there was Papa and his little family trees. He worked so hard on them. He was probably getting worried by now. He said he always prayed for his only granddaughter.

Dot rolled up the window. "We're going to get you home," she said. "Your hair's going to need a good brushing."

Dot tossed her phone onto the passenger floorboard by Ramona's dainty slippered feet. An Oregon State Police officer sailed past them on the other side of the highway. She was following the rules, right? Not speeding. Ten and two. No, three and nine. Is this considered a kidnapping?

She exited, signaling and braking 200 feet before, like Dad taught her. She pulled into a Shell and parked, picked up her phone. For a split second, she thought about posing for a selfie with Ramona and sending that to Zoe for shock value. But that wouldn't be right, and you know what Zoe would do. As much as Dot hated when Dad said it, the little phrase reminding her of a sex act, Zoe was actually rubbing off on Dot, and it probably wasn't a good thing. She instead called everyone to let them know she was safe, that she was coming back.

She almost called Zoe, but Dot thought it better to just keep this to herself. She wouldn't even tell her friend that she took Dad's truck down the highway. It was probably time to stop telling Zoe everything.

Dot might tell Rick about this, though. After she got to know him more. If they ever officially went out, he'd just have to accept that her family was a little odd. That Papa and Dad lived in small houses. That her step-grandma was latex. Maybe Rick's people weren't like Mom's people, always judging you in silence. It was funny how, instead of relatives, Papa called them *your people*.

POWER HOUR

Day 6

Breakfast

—banana smoothie

—handful of walnuts

—½ grapefruit

—½ cup dry granola (not so bad now)

Laurette woke me up again this morning. She's so thin, I worry she'll fly away. She comes over all fresh and bright in tight clothes, but I can tell she's exhausted. I bet she only gets a few hours of sleep a night. Skinny people are freakish like that.

Yesterday's appearance by Christopher Campbell was one of two this week. If we make it past the first seven days, we'll be seeing a lot of him. That's the enticement. Since I paid for a Personal Power Hour, I'll be seeing him sooner than that. I'm still a little star struck and just plain nervous. What will I say to him?

So far, four out of the 50 people that started have left. Two were in the same van I rode coming in. Sandy from Phoenix left Wednesday morning. She was a sweet girl. Charlie from Houston left too. I liked him. Not bad looking either. After the first workout and that awful "BBQ," he told me he could never be a vegan because he loved Arby's too much, talking about all those layers of thin meat and sweet sauce. He's such a funny guy. Sad he's gone.

Lunch

—grilled asparagus, green beans, zucchini, portabella mushroom over rice noodles

—green salad with lemon juice and salt (yuck-o!)

Dinner

—pearled basil couscous

—spinach soup with pine nuts

—peppermint tea

Day 7

Breakfast

—kiwifruit, pineapple

—granola cereal with milk (this I can do, even though it's soy milk)

—almonds

The tropical fruit reminded me of Hawaii. That was the best trip. Daddy's last before he got too big to travel. I wish I could go back, just to that time with Momma and Daddy so happy. They kept saying thank you, thank you for the trip, and I admit: I was pretty proud to have paid for everything. My first real gift to them as an adult. I owe them everything. Oh, Daddy, I miss you.

They try to make this place like paradise, with the palm trees and pools and trendy decor, but it's far from tropical. The only way this place is an island is the grassy-carpeted perimeter that fends off the ocean of thorny shrubs and hot sand in all directions. It amazes me how the desert doesn't just creep all the way inside, but then I think maybe it has, because the mood here kills.

Tomorrow we *Turn the Corner!* and renew our Harmony Health Center Life Contracts. We also have our second Team Power Hour with Christopher. Maybe this time I'll actually listen rather than stare at him.

Lunch

—green salad, no dressing

—veggie burger on sprouted-wheat bun (nasty!)

—baked sweet potato fries (pretty good)

More exercise this afternoon. Forty minutes on the treadmill, followed by calisthenics. By the end of it, my feet hurt so bad I wanted to cry. Lisa from Pittsburgh—my neighbor across the hall—did. She just sat down and wailed. They had to come lift her up and walk her out. It was horrible.

Dinner

—Japanese eggplant stir-fry

—vegetable spring roll in rice paper (GROSS!)

Day 8

My butt is sore and I miss my own bed. Today was a cleanse. No food to write about other than watermelon water, miso soup, carrot juice, celery juice, and enough herbal tea and water to fill the Gulf of Mexico. I thought I would be raging all day, but the smoothies helped. The mentors say if you drink enough water, you'll feel full and won't want to eat anyway. I don't buy that.

Laurette says she only drinks water with lemon and a dash of salt on her cleanse days. Today, she looked like she might pass out. Her skin was pale, and her hands were shaking. I thought she might have been charged up on caffeine. She brought me a Before and After pic of CC.

"You're working on your After pic as we speak," she said. She had just run four miles and wanted to be the first to congratulate me for making it through the first week.

I asked her why she was once heavy, and she said she didn't take care of herself. She put her hands on her waist and waited for me to say something, maybe for me to agree with her. Later she came to say good night and told me to keep on going. She hugged me, and when she left, it felt like a wispy spirit had floated out of my room.

Day 9

I woke up this morning to two awful things: a pounding headache and Stu, another mentor. He looked like the rest of the staff in his blue Harmony Health polo shirt and track pants, but he was pushy and his hair was way too perfect. He didn't smile and his news was even worse: Laurette is no longer with HHC. *Personal reasons. I'm your new mentor.* He tapped his watch and left.

Breakfast

—berry medley w/ walnuts

—granola cereal w/ soy yogurt (yuck)

—green tea (it's the closest thing to coffee I'll get around here)

I ate alone at Nutrition Central worrying about Laurette. Maybe she was fired? Last year when they announced we were acquired by Fitzsimmons, they said the integration would be quick, and within a few months we'd know where we stood. I survived the first cuts, thank God. I was surprised. Senior managers are usually the first to go, senior marketing managers at that. Others weren't as lucky. When clients called and asked for someone who was laid off, we were told to say they are no longer with the company. That was that.

Lunch
—green salad
—spicy lentil soup
—date spread on whole-grain bread

Dinner
—vegetarian enchiladas (with real cheese from a GOAT!—I'm not complaining though)
—cornbread

Day 10
Breakfast
—blueberries
—steel-cut oatmeal
—green tea

I've dropped eight pounds since I've been here. I'm super proud of that. Stu, however, calls them my "second chance" pounds. He gives me articles and charts and wants to see my journal. He's trying to distract me so I don't miss Laurette. At workouts and group talks, he says I'm doing a great job in front of everyone, but I can tell when a guy is pretending to be nice.

At lunch, I asked him about Christopher Campbell, since my Power Hour is tomorrow. Stu called him "The Master." Enjoy every minute, he said. He picked up his tray and caught up to Michelle and Robin, two cutesy mentors who I'm sure never had a chubby past.

Lunch

—turkey sandwich on wheat bread (yes! some meat! and so delicious)

—cucumber slices

—assorted nuts

I can't sleep. I'm worried about Laurette. I wish there was a way to talk to her. She's the only person who seems real around here. I know I'm making progress, so I'm going to stick with it. Maybe Christopher's the only other real person in here. Oh my God, I meet with him tomorrow! Maybe our private Power Hour will turn into a date, and over the table I'll see those lonely eyes I saw in his Before pic, the ones that sucked me in on Day I, just before he busted through his life-size picture and bounded on stage, the new and improved CC.

Day II

Last entry. This one's for you, Laurette. Be strong, if you can.

I'm back in my room and it's late. After lunch, I locked myself in and skipped dinner. I'm not hungry. Maybe that's the point of meeting with The Master: he'll make you so horribly sick you'll never want to eat again.

Stu and Penny Colby—the program director of Harmony—knocked on my door and practically demanded they come in. I told them both to leave me the F alone, and I shouted through the door that this program's a sham. I'm suing the place for negligence, I said. I'm packing my things and will be expecting a full refund.

I just packed my bathroom stuff and remembered some advice Barbara Reeves, the dietician at SMU, once gave me. She said, "Look at yourself every day and say: *'Olivia, I love you, I've always loved you, and I will support everything you do.'*" They've taught nothing of this sort at Harmony.

Before I go, lunch. My Power Hour.

I sat at a glass patio table set for two in a private garden behind the Nutrition Central building. The sky was bright blue, and it wasn't God-awful hot. I did some Power Breathing to calm my jitters, but then a young female staffer I'd never seen walked over. She stood there waiting for me with a glass of water with lemon and a dash of salt.

"Isn't it a beautiful day?" she said.

"Yes. Yes it is." Behind her perfect skin and hair, I caught a flash of L.A.'s brown halo infiltrating the valley. When I landed two weeks ago, it looked like we were descending into a big dirty cough and I thought, no way, no how, would you ever see *that* in Dallas.

"Christopher will be with you shortly," she said.

I sipped the cool lemony water and tried to think of nothing, but then he appeared. He didn't walk toward me or from behind; he just stood there, out of nowhere. My throat tightened and I tugged at my HHC bracelet. I stood up to greet him and my knees wobbled.

The whites of his eyes and blue pupils sparkled. His teeth shined against his tan skin and short, glossy hair. I wanted to touch him to see if he was real.

"Olivia?" He gave me his hand. It overtook mine and he shook it once, then smiled his name. *Christopher Campbell.* He motioned for me to sit, but I froze and felt big and awkward.

"Pleased to meet you," I said.

"Likewise. So tell me about yourself," he said.

I had hardly given him the basics before he shifted right into the hard questions: *How long have you been living as a large person? Have you always been overweight? Did a traumatic incident cause you to gain weight? Were you modeling another person's behavior; say, a family member's?*

He leaned in when he talked, and I felt him scanning me all over; like he was sizing me up, figuring how he was going to make me small. Then the food came. He grinned and seemed to forget the questions.

Lunch
—green salad
—vegetarian chili
—whole grain crisps
—olive tapenade

I started eating and kept quiet.

"Olivia, I want to congratulate you," he said, "on your progress so far here at Harmony Health Center. I'm thrilled that you decided to meet with me today. That means you're committed to change." He flashed another smile.

I looked down into my chili and suddenly hated the food more than ever. I tried again to replace his plastic face with the one in the Before pic. I wanted the mystery man.

He said, "Let me tell you a story, Olivia. A few years ago, I was a top performer at my job. I traveled; had fancy dinners, cocktails; belonged to airline clubs; had disposable income, an expense account, you name it. I rubbed elbows with the bosses, pleased clients—all the good stuff they say will make you a star. But while I was doing all those so-called good things, I wasn't taking care of myself. I was trying to be the best and rewarded myself only with decadence. I started distancing myself from my family and friends, and I even avoided romantic relationships. You probably know exactly what I was going through, don't you, Olivia?"

I wanted a hug from my Daddy right then. Just one more.

"A stomach ulcer landed me in the hospital. The doctors said my LDL cholesterol was 242 and my blood pressure was 159 over 95. Do you know what that means, Olivia?"

Of course I knew. Daddy ticked around like that for a long time. When his bomb went off, just four months ago, there was no way to turn it back.

"The docs said, at the rate I was going, I better start planning for an early funeral. Olivia, at thirty-six years old, I was over two-hundred pounds and my body age was fifty-two!"

I had heard this same speech before. Late one night on Christopher's hour-long infomercial, he pointed at me and said: "Make the commitment to yourself!"

Christopher slammed the table with both hands. The ceramic plates and silverware clanged on the glass top. "Then I woke up," he said. "I got out of the hospital, stopped eating junk, and lowered my portion sizes. I started walking and began to sweat away all the poison. That was when I started walking the path to health. And that's the path you're on right now, Olivia."

All I could muster was a weak smile. "Are you happier now?" I asked.

He grinned and leaned closer. I felt the hard sell coming on. "May I show you something?" he said.

He stood and untucked his polo shirt and lifted it up. His stomach was firm but crisscrossed with long lines and deep staple marks. He looked down at his mutilated abdominals and repeated my question. "Am I happier now? Look at me. I'm the happiest I've ever been in my life!"

When our company's salesmen would come in for their QBRs, they always had these sharp suits and ties with their tanned carved faces, like they just got back from vacation. They only talked to the girls in reception, or some of the girls on my team, like Melinda and Georgia. They'd take them out to drinks after work and never invite me. Me. The boss.

The inside of my chest caved, felt like it was rolling in on itself. I felt that when Daddy died, and more recently when I thought about Laurette. Something bad had happened. I knew it.

And so I asked him: "What happened to Laurette?"

Christopher sat back and tapped the table. The red and gold HHC bracelet, like the one on my wrist, looked wrong on his, like he had just put it on right before we met.

"It's not good," he said. "She's let her disorder take over."

I looked down at the chili in front of me and tried not to gag. I stood. My knees buckled.

"What happened?" I said. "Is she——?"

"Almost," he said. "Please sit."

"You're sick," I said. "You people are sick."

"It's a disease, Olivia. Just like overeating. You have a disease too. But you're on the path," he said.

I've never been a violent person. Never punched or slapped anyone. The most I did was probably in middle school when I shoved a girl named Circe into a locker. It was right after choir, and Mrs. Harmon had just given me the solo for the Christmas program. I was practically flying with joy. Then I bumped into Circe and she called me Wide Load in front of all of her stupid friends. All that happiness twisted up, and something jumped inside me, like a little devil. When Circe's back hit the yellow metal door, her friends giggled. Circe turned bright red. I could have ripped down a wall that day.

I grabbed the bowl of chili and threw it at CC. It hit his lap and the red goop plopped up onto his chin and blue polo. The bowl bounced and hit the bricks and busted into three sharp pieces.

Christopher wiped his face with the white cloth napkin. He locked in on me, and I saw them—those sad, lonely eyes. He put the napkin down, and I thought for a second: Maybe he was still somewhere inside there. Then he said, "Nice going, Olivia."

I pictured him stuck there forever, always trying to keep his teeth white and his shirt clean, trying to forget his Before picture. But it didn't matter if he was fat or fit, he'd always be the same person, all the way down to the bone.

I yanked the HHC bracelet off my wrist and tossed it on the table, and somehow felt lighter than ever. I think I know now exactly how to keep that feeling going. It doesn't have a taste or a shape, and I don't have to pay for it or ask someone to say it for me. Not now, not ever.

RATTLESNAKE RABBIT

LOVING A HYPOCHONDRIAC has its perks. For one, you learn about all kinds of sicknesses and how to treat them. When Nadine diagnosed herself with Celiac Disease, we threw out all the carbs and started eating Paleo. She lost some weight, then after the tests came back negative, it turned out she was just tired and needed more sleep.

The other day it was, "Do you feel this lump? Is it hard or soft? Can you move it around with your fingers? Palpate it. Please."

"It's probably nothing bad," I tell her. "I mean, you can move it. See?"

And she'll say, "I'm going to make an appointment anyway. Just to rule things out."

Things being the really bad stuff. I don't say it at all because I don't want to give it anything. That's how my people are. We don't want to send the wrong message to the Spirit by looking all that stuff up. We don't dwell on it unless we want something from it. Not Nadine's people. They think about it all day and night until they have an answer. They go get tests and more tests.

Today, I'm meeting her at her gynecologist's office. I get a little nervous when she goes there because what if it turns out she's pregnant? We've been a little careless here and there, sometimes not following the calendar exactly with her cycles. She won't use birth control because of all the chemicals and doesn't want to have more female problems down the line, with all the hormones. And because she's Catholic. I always laugh to myself though because if she was so Catholic, she wouldn't have me practically living at her place the way I do, keeping a set of everything over there, and me going home on Saturday mornings to get more stuff. We'll probably get married one of these days, but that will mean a long process with my tribe.

We meet in this medical center's beautiful lobby that reminds me of what the Hanging Gardens of Babylon must have looked like if it were indoors and in downtown San Diego. I usually like meeting here because it's so pretty, but she comes out of her doctor's office and her eyebrows are pinched together.

"What is it? Something's wrong."

"My Pap is abnormal."

"What does that mean?"

"It's precancerous."

"For real, for real?"

"Yes, for real. I'm positive for HPV. I don't know for how long."

"Well, how? Why?"

"From sex," she says. "With you."

"How?"

"I must have gotten HPV from you."

"I don't know that I have that. What is that even?"

"See? You never go to the doctor. You don't know what's going on with your body. You don't know what you're giving to people."

When Nadine tried out for Miss California, her platform was disease prevention. She focused on simple techniques like soaking your toothbrush in hydrogen peroxide every now and then, or changing the hand towels out often in your bathroom to prevent the spread of germs. Prevention is the best cure, it's the best cure for everyone, was her little tagline. Something she said she picked up in a sixth-grade play where she was the star.

"You think I gave this to you? On purpose? You're the one that doesn't want me to wear something when we—"

"Just stop," she says. "I have to come back next week so they can do the colposcopy."

"What's that?"

"Go look it up." She moves past me. "No, you know what? Why don't you go talk to the elders, or go smoke out and ask the spirit what it is?"

She walks out the sliding glass doors, and I scream right there in the Hanging Gardens. A lady sticks her head out of one of the offices on the first floor, and the lobby receptionist stands and picks up the phone. I walk out the other door.

NADINE AND I first met in the coffee shop in the casino. I was on break from working security at the V Lounge. Bonnie Raitt was playing, and Nadine was there to see her. It was a mellow night. Nothing usually happens at shows there. But then in walks Nadine and some of her friends and she was flirting and I was open to anything.

We poured it all out in a matter of days after our first date, which was only sitting and having coffee. She went right into how her parents were high-functioning alcoholics, said how there was some hitting and a lot of yelling and criticizing all the way up into college. That was when she started smoking pot and trying other things like cocaine, plus, she was eating a lot. She said she also drank, but not like her parents. I never knew there was such a thing as a high-functioning alcoholic. I had an uncle that died from too much booze.

My story was a like a TV show compared to hers. Kumeyaay reservation boy. Stable parents, grandparents, cousins, relatives (except for the taint of my uncle) and a happy home. I worked hard in school and was a wrestler. Never tried a drop of anything and still haven't. Nadine is the most dangerous girl I ever dated. And it's why I'm so hot for her. Plus, me being with her is more or less forbidden.

I'm not supposed to be with white girls, and Nadine is like really white. Blonde, fair skin like a Scandinavian, and blue eyes. Blue eyes, they say, will eventually go away. They're recessive and it's people like Nadine breeding with other Nadine-like people that will keep them going. She's somewhat tall, about as tall as me, and she's a solid, healthy woman, not at all bone-skinny like the models you see today.

Among her almost-illnesses, Nadine is always trying to find some new diet. She really did try the Viking diet of strictly fish and vegetables, and lost some weight, and then she started complaining that no matter what she does, she'll never be as thin as me, and that I hardly have to do anything before you can start to see my muscles. I tell her she's beautiful the way she is, and that maybe she shouldn't try so hard. She usually brushes that off.

It's true she gets all her self-confidence from the pageants though. They're expensive, but they're the only way she builds herself up. In the ten months we've been together, she's done at least five of them, including the big one that she won a couple months ago. When she comes back from them, she's like a new woman. No symptoms of disease of any kind, no mean talk, no issues with eating. She's like the perfect girl. If she could permanently be in a pageant, she'd be the best. I think it's what they do at pageants. They pump each other up and it's not really like competing. It's just all those girls being princesses is all.

But there I go, saying what I wish she could be. That's wrong. I love her and want her the way she is. I'm serious about that.

She texts me later, starts off by saying she won't be at her apartment tonight, so don't come over.

Where are you going? I ask.

She replies: My Mom's.

This is not good. When Nadine goes to her mom's place, a few things happen, a long chain reaction that only messes her up. But she goes back because—and this is how it starts—she tries to use some of her pageant empowerment techniques on her mom, about how to be strong and independent and not rely on bad things like food or men or drugs and alcohol, then that tips her mom off to start trying to justify the past.

What Nadine is really doing though, is trying to hide from her own problems, which makes her mom just push harder on Nadine, and so begins this back and forth struggle where her mom makes some food, and they eat, and then they keep eating, and talking, and trying to empower, and trying to bring down, and crying and more eating, until Nadine's really in a pit. Not to mention Nadine's mom has six or seven cats in her small place, which stirs up Nadine's allergies. Once, she stayed the night over there and she couldn't breathe, almost had to sleep on the balcony.

All I can text back is: Do you have your inhaler?

Got it, she writes back. Good night.

I know all this because Nadine tells me what goes on there, and with her psychology degree, she lays it out like a case study. I've actually never met her mom. I know her name's Lydia. Her mom doesn't come to the pageants, never out to dinner with us, and she's never been to Nadine's. I have this little nagging thought that Nadine hasn't told her mom I'm

Native. The way she describes her mom as a judgmental witch—Nadine's words—I don't think she'd take kindly to an Indian boy.

Oh, well. I'm going over there tonight anyway. There's a letter here at Nadine's place from the American Beauties Plus Pageant. It could be something good. I mean, she is Miss California. They might want her to do something. She might have to reign over something, or be in a parade maybe. She's been talking about the national pageant a lot. The one in Orlando later this year.

AT THE TRADER Joe's on the way out to Lakeside I pick up a bouquet of hydrangeas. Nadine loves blue hydrangeas. They last a while if they've got some good sun and lots of water. But don't keep them in the fridge to make them last longer. They'll burn. She tried that once when she was having an appearance and signing autographs at this health fair. She wanted them at her table. I had put the flowers in her fridge the night before thinking they would stay fresh, but by the next morning, the little blue petals had all turned brown. She was furious.

I found her mom's address from the Valentine card she sent. This year's was handmade, like they always are, but this one seemed more thrown together than usual. It was bright red and shiny and glued on the front were a pair of fuzzy slippers. Not sure if those were meant to be a reminder of what her mom is like, or what her mom might want for Valentine's. Nadine said, "This is so my mother," when she had opened the card. I really don't get that holiday.

Outside Nadine's mom's place, a little porch light flickers above her duplex number, and I think of Rabbit. He'd gone away from his hole, and while he was gone, a rattlesnake went inside. When Rabbit came back, he had a feeling something wasn't right. So instead of going right into his hole, he knocked first, and sure enough, the rattlesnake answered, "Hello?"

Right before I knock, I have that same feeling. My Grandfather, after he told that story asked, "What did Rabbit do there?"

"He knocked," I would say.

"No," Grandfather said. "He listened to his gut."

My gut is saying I should go. I have the feeling that Nadine calls the heebie-jeebies. My real gut is saying to knock and get my girlfriend. Rescue her. But then, does she need rescuing? Whenever she's in the slumps about her weight, or her new thought-up illness, I think to myself that all she needs to do is stop thinking about it.

I knock. There's a voice, a yip it sounds like. Feet walking to the door. It opens.

Nadine has shown me pictures of her family, and they surprise me every time. They too look a little thrown together. Tall dad, short mom, dark haired thin boy, blonde big girl. I guess that's why Nadine said she felt like she never belonged. She often said she wished she was adopted so she wouldn't have to claim them. Our people, it's hard to tell where the families end and begin, we all look so alike.

Her mother in those pictures stood a few feet below everyone else and seemed harmless. Though in her eyes, even in those pictures, you could tell her mind was clouded. She reminded me of the old-time pictures of white people where nobody smiled. They just sat or stood there for hours and hours trying to be dignified, but they ended up looking pretty pissed off, their souls captured by the camera. That's why you never see us lining up for family portraits.

She opens the door, and yes, she's shorter, but I do feel intimidated, like when you see a spider or scorpion. Grandfather would say your rabbit sense tells you they are dangerous, yet they are creatures too with a soul, and they only turn if you provoke them.

"Is Nadine here?"

Her mom's nervous, a little shaky. She is wearing sweatpants, her hair short and choppy. Two yellow and striped cats saunter in the doorway next to her.

"Who are you?" She keeps the door almost closed.

"I'm Ron. Nadine's boyfriend."

She scans me up and down. I've seen Nadine make those same troubled eyes.

"I thought you'd be the ambulance," she says, peeking out, trying to look around me.

"The ambulance? Why?"

"Nadine's in a bad way," she says.

"Where is she?" I push on the door. One of the cats steps over the threshold and I don't know what makes Nadine's mom more upset, me trying to come in, or the cat trying to leave. She tries to stop us both, and I can feel this woman is capable of force. Nadine said her mom never struck her regularly as much as she screamed like a banshee. That banshee woman—another scary legend Nadine's people have.

"You get out." Nadine's mom pushes back with the strength of Rattlesnake. Rabbit is quick. It's the only way he escapes Rattlesnake. That, and he's smarter.

Inside her place, the other cats pace, some sit on the table where there's a bottle of beer and a pie with a few slices

85

missing, and the TV is on but no sound comes from it. Nadine is on the couch, asleep. Two cats keep a watch over her on top of the cushions. I rush to her, take her hand. She's limp and pasty. Her skin is cool.

"What happened? When did you call the ambulance?" I turn back. Nadine's mom rushes behind me, I think to try to move me, but she scoops up a yellow cat and holds it in her arms like a baby.

"That girl always thinks she has something." Nadine's mom caresses its belly. "Are you Indian? You're an Indian, aren't you?"

Nadine's chest rises. She's breathing, but it's far apart. "Tell me what happened."

Nadine's mom points to the side table. A prescription bottle and a glass of water sit under the light of a blue lamp. The pill bottle is closed, and the label says phenobarbital with the name, "McCallister, Lydia."

"These are yours."

"They're for my anxiety." Nadine's mom—Lydia—lets her cat down and comes toward me, reaching for the bottle. "She came over here all in a panic about her Pap smear and cancer and—you don't know this girl. She panics about everything. So I gave—here, give me those pills—" Lydia grabs them from me, tucks them in her pocket. "Girl's had some kind of death wish since she was small."

I watch Nadine like I do in the morning before she wakes up. She never got to sleep late because her dad was up early making noise, guilty from a hangover. He'd wake them by pulling the blinds and covers off them. In the mornings while she sleeps, I go make the foods she likes: eggs, sausage, toast, and juice, and I think of how lucky I am to have such a woman.

I could, and often do, get lost in her. Nadine's chest stops moving. I check her pulse. She's still in there.

It all comes back to me: thirty chest compressions, head back, rescue breath. First, I lean in and kiss her, ask the Spirit to keep her here, tell her I'm sorry if it was me that gave her this, and that she'll be fine. And I leave it at that. I don't go back to that thought. I move on to the second round. I clasp together and push hard on her chest. *Twenty-eight, twenty-nine, thirty.* Chin back, breath in. Again. And again. It was one of the first things they taught us in the two-day security training way back when. I paid attention.

Knocks at the door don't distract me, though I can hear them. Radiant below me is my American Beauty, surrounded by the cats, spirits themselves. I ask for their blessing.

In rush the men in uniforms and they don't push me aside. They let me work. Another round, my fourth. I go hard on the fifth. They settle in beside me, one taking vitals, the other readjusting her. A third, I sense, behind me, has the gurney open and ready. *Twenty-eight, twenty-nine, thirty.* A flutter of eyelids? Lydia comes closer, kneels next to me. Her hand clutching my shoulder I do feel. The paramedics, without words, take over.

They rush to the door and one turns back to us—motions to Mrs. Lydia and me. Come with us, he's saying. Everything is quiet like the TV. The cats stay frozen where they are. Nadine on the stretcher is out the door. I glance back at the kitchen table debating to bring the hydrangeas. I doubt Mrs. Lydia will care for them, but I leave them anyway. Maybe she'll change. Wake up, I ask. Wake up.

IN THE ER waiting room, I wait. Feels like hours, but it's only been about one. Lydia went in, next of kin. I had to stay out here. On my phone, I scroll through some pictures, mostly of Nadine alone or in her dresses on stage, or on our dates where we take pictures of our food. There's a few of us together. There's one where she's holding the camera out, kissing me, but me trying to fight being in the picture. She had said, "Gotcha!" when she took that one.

I'm trying so hard not to let the bad thought come back. *Change thoughts, change thoughts.* Don't give more bad energy to your worries. Be strong. Grandpa said crying only shows weakness. Only gives it more. I forgot that crying starts as a choking feeling in your throat, and you can't stop it. The gush begins and the bad thoughts flood in, too—that she might stay out there forever. She's been distant even before the gynecologist.

The big automatic door opens. Lydia and a nurse come out, no expressions. Lydia waves to me to follow her. The nurse helps usher me down the hall. ERs feel worse when you're there for someone else. It's like the passageway between life and death, the moaning, and beeping, the smell of no smell, and the clocks, stuck in time.

"She's asking for you," the nurse says.

The choking almost returns to my throat. Lydia nods her head, taps my arm like when a stranger taps you, and they're trying to get to know you.

"She's going to make it," Lydia says. "She always does."

Nadine's bed is elevated a bit, and she's got an IV in her hand. Her monitors show a beating heart. She's asleep. I rush to her, grab her hand. She squeezes. I lean down to kiss her, and my choking comes back. My tears roll off my nose and onto her face. She opens her eyes. She's in there. Her spirit is coming back. I'm never going to let it out of my sight. I'm going to protect it like a dream. Hold onto it by telling it to myself over and again so it never fades.

BAT OUT OF HELL

MARGARET ASSURES HERSELF: leaving Mom here, at an OXXO convenience store at Benito Juárez and Constitución, a few miles deep into Tijuana, is just like Mom used to do to her as a little girl. Except then, it was in New Mexico, in their hometown of Clayton. Mom would drive Margaret and her sisters down First Street, promising them a Slush Puppy, but when they'd get to Allsup's, Mom only gave enough money for a pack of Newports, and she always sent Margaret, the youngest, in to get them. Margaret would come out with the cigarettes, standing alone in front of the store, cars gassing up, the street so far away, to find no Bel Air with Mom, Joana, and Tina. They'd left her there, like a dog, as Mom would say. Then after a while they'd barrel back around the block, laughing their heads off, Mom in charge of it all.

"Get in," she'd say. "And quit crying."

Now, in front of the OXXO, under a darkening sky, Margaret considers locking the doors and scrapping the whole deal. This will ensure her a direct ticket to hell, but she'd get her life back in return.

"Mom." Margaret taps her sleeping mother's shoulder. "We're here."

Mom comes to. "Where?" she says.

"We're getting some sandwiches. Go on in. I'll park."

"But look at me," Mom says. "I don't have my face on."

Classic Mom: always thinking one day she'll be discovered.

"Just go inside. What are you getting? Turkey? Roast beef?" Margaret says.

Mom opens the passenger door, sets a slippered foot on foreign pavement.

"Go ahead." Margaret's guts twist up. "I'll meet you."

This shouldn't be how it ends. Yet it was either Mom goes or Margaret's family goes. Even her son Cameron said it, bless his little heart. "When's Grandma going home?"

"Shut the door, Mom," Margaret says. "I'll be right back, okay?"

Mom closes the door. Margaret rolls down the window. "Go on."

Mom shuffles up to the front door and pushes. She looks back once more at the minivan. "Roast beef," she says.

"Good. Me too." Margaret rolls up the window, nods once with resolve and a growing lump in her throat. She presses down on the gas.

THE ODYSSEY ZIPS over bumps in the boulevard and dodges two fast cars turning into her lane. She lays on her wimpy horn at the pink taillights stopped for no reason. She speeds back up under street signs she can read, but barely understand, her Spanish all but gone. Mom's always criticizing her for that. *Garita*, Margaret knows, is the border crossing.

She shakes her head. People are going to ask, "Where'd your mom go?"

Oh, I took her back home. What? Oh, no. She doesn't live with us full-time. She's just visiting from New Mexico. Where I grew up. You see, her home isn't my home. My home

*is my home. Mine and my husband Eric's, and my daughter
Lacey and my son Cameron's home. Just ours. All ours.*

Margaret steers onto a northbound highway. *Is this it?*
She blasts some cold air, shivers after a few seconds, then turns
it to heat. *Too hot. Oh, God, Oh, God, I had to. I was going
to kill her otherwise. I could have pushed her down the stairs.
Choked her. Suffocated her. Mixed up all those meds to give
her one hell of a forever-nap. Shit, I could have drowned her
in our pool. Made them all look like innocent little accidents.
No, officer, I just found her face down, floating there. This
was better. More humane. By now, Mom probably realizes
she's not in San Diego.*

Right up until Margaret had had it, Mom was on a loop
with that story about her and Margaret's alien abduction. The
kids thought it was cute for a while.

"Again, Grandma, again!" they'd shout.

"It was late," Mom would start. "The movie ended and
all the cars had gone home. It was just me and Midge at the
drive-in. I had to clean the snack bar, so I told Midge to go
play outside. I finished cleaning and emptied the till."

"What's the till, Grandma?"

"Cash register."

"Then I called Grandpa—*que Dios le bendiga*—to tell
him we were on our way back to town. It would only take
fifteen minutes, no more than that."

And she'd get quiet then. It was how she told all her
stories, to hook you in, but those last few times, when she
started going on repeat mode, her silence between beats was
more her getting lost in her own lie, the eroding of the story
she'd been working on her whole life.

"We left the drive-in at eleven o'clock," she'd say.

"Why was Mommy out so late?" the kids would ask.

"Things were different back then. It was the summer. And a hot one at that."

"Then what happened?" they'd ask.

"I drove on the Texline highway toward Clayton in the pitch dark. Not a car in front of us, not a car behind us. Midge was in the back, taking a nap."

And the kids would cackle—one, at their own mother's nickname, and two, at the fact that she could take a nap at eleven o'clock at night. Midge, Mom said, was a cute form of Margaret, but really it was for midget, Margaret being the shortest of the three girls.

"Then, all in a sudden, a light, the brightest light I ever seen, brighter than a thousand flashlights, flooded the Bel Air. It was so bright I had to hide my eyes. I gripped the steering wheel and pumped the brakes, but I couldn't stop the car. It was like the car didn't work at all. Then the car started to shake and jerk forward."

Mom shimmied her torso, her ample breasts swaying for effect. The kids were both riveted and disturbed.

"Midge woke up and shouted, 'What is it, what is it?'"

"What was it, Mom?" the kids would ask. "Did you scream?"

"She was too young to remember," Mom would say. And Margaret agreed with her, a willing accomplice to the legend, but actually, she had no memory of it at all. Margaret had been eight, maybe nine years old, and the only lights on that lonely highway were truckers trying to get back to Texas as fast as they could.

"And then all in a sudden—"

"It's all *of* a sudden, Grandma. All *of* a sudden," the kids would say.

"Then all of a sudden, the light disappeared!" Mom slapped her hands together. "And—just like that!—the light was gone. I got control of the car again and drove like a bat out of Hell back to Clayton. Me and Midgey cried all the way home."

The kids would look to their mother for validation. "Then what, then what?"

They knew the payoff, but they waited for Mom to say it with that faraway look in her eyes, the look she was no longer faking in recent months.

"We pulled into the driveway, and Grandpa came running outside to meet us. I held Midge in my arms—she had fallen back asleep. Grandpa hugged and kissed us like he thought he would never see us again.

"'Where have you been?' he said.

"'In the car. On the highway. We saw a bright—' I tried to tell him, but he pulled us into the kitchen and showed us the clock.

"'It's two in the morning!' he said. 'It's been three hours since you called!'"

The kids would grab at each other.

"And that was it. We didn't remember anything. We don't know what flew over the car, or where we went for three hours," she'd say.

"Was it a plane? A helicopter? Was it a U—?"

"Shhh, shhh, shhh, don't say it. I don't want to think about it. The only thing I know is both me and Midge have this little mole right here on our necks that we never had before that night."

Her finishing touch to the story. She'd point to the tiny raised freckle at the back of her neck, right side, far behind her ear, nestled in the nape of her short old-lady haircut.

"Show yours, Mom," the kids would scream.

And Margaret would lift her hair to show hers. Sure, it was identical. But they're mother and daughter. They're going to have some similarities.

"Was it like where they—" Always from Lacey, taking it a step further.

"Shhh, shhh. I don't want to know," Mom would say.

I don't want to know. I don't want to know. Margaret gets off at an intersection now less than a mile from the border. The crush of cars reminds her why she hasn't been to Tijuana in at least eight years. A young homeless woman and her three small children walk through the idling cars, the mother shaking a cup. A man in a beat-up tracksuit smacks Margaret's windshield with his hand, begins spraying it with a bottle of brownish liquid, then wipes it with a small squeegee.

"No, no, no!" Margaret waves her finger at him. The light turns green. She brings that finger to the mole on the back of her neck and pulls ahead.

SHE INCHES FORWARD, still on the Mexico side. Vendors push rugs, sodas, tamarindos, and chicharrones at her. *No, no, no, no gracias.* She wishes she had a cigarette. Just once in a while isn't going to kill you. But that was so much like Mom. Margaret fiddles with the radio dials. Every channel crystal-clear this close to all the towers, but nothing worth listening to. Not on a Sunday night. Ten minutes turns into an hour.

She approaches the Customs and Border Patrol officers. Nothing to worry about. No drugs. No merchandise. She breathes. Practices her speech.

—*What were you doing in Mexico?*

Just visiting some relatives.

—*How long were you there?*

Half a day.

—*Where are you from?*

Oceanside.

More vendors claw at her car. *No, no, no.* She waves her finger. One last try to get a buck.

Margaret pulls up to the booth, rolls down her window. The officer peers inside.

"Nationality?" he asks.

"U.S."

"Traveling alone?" he says.

"Yes."

"Passport."

Margaret fumbles through her purse, almost grabs her mother's passport. On the way into Mexico, she'd whispered a story to the officer. "She's been sick. We're trying to get her down to see her cousins. She's really tired."

The officer almost hadn't let her pass with a sleeping passenger, but the two U.S. passports made him more lenient. "Have a safe trip," the officer had said. Mom snored on, head tilted back, mouth wide open.

Now, the officer hands back Margaret's passport.

"Ma'am," he says, eyes steely and steady, "please pull ahead and to the right for further inspection."

She complies. *Further inspection? They're not keeping records, are they? No. No, no, no, no. They do this to all Hispanics. Yes, of course they do. They just have to check.*

An officer sidles up to her window in the secondary inspection zone. Mom left nothing in the car. No bag. No shoes. Margaret checks her phone. The screen says: Welcome to Mexico. International rates apply.

"Ma'am, please step out of your vehicle and wait over there by the curb."

She gets out of the car. The officers open doors, look under seats.

Margaret rubs her neck, runs her finger over her mole.

An officer approaches Margaret, stone-faced. "All clear, ma'am. Please proceed."

"Was there something wrong?" she asks.

"No. Just your car. Minivans."

Margaret rubs her neck. California twinkles in the distance.

"Let me take another look at your passport," he says.

She takes it out, hands it to him.

"Ruth Velasquez?" he says.

"Oh, sorry." She rifles through her bag. "Here, this one."

"Whose was that?"

"My mother's."

"And where is she?"

"In Mexico. She's staying. I'm coming back down to get her. I just forgot to give it to her."

"That's pretty important to have when you're in Mexico," he says.

"Gosh, I know. I'm so stupid."

She smiles the smile Mom taught her and her sisters a long time ago. When confronted by a man, especially Daddy, smile like you're shy. They melt every time.

He reviews her document, scans her up and down, glances back at her car.

"Okay," he says. "Have a safe trip."

Margaret gets back in, fires the engine. Interstate 5 is just ahead, past the series of colossal speed bumps. *What do I tell Eric and the kids? I drove Mom as far as Arizona. Yes, that's where Aunt Joana picked Mom up. Yeah. And for Joana and Tina? Okay, Mom went for a walk one afternoon and she never came back. You know she was starting to slip. You know she was starting to need more of the meds. Forgetting having been to places. Repeating stories. It was only a matter of time. Oh, who cares? Joana and Tina don't even call to check in on her. They sent her out to me because I'm the youngest. They were done with Mom's bullshit a long time ago.*

The cars move ahead and the wide lanes of Califorriia's artery open, pumping them back into circulation. Red and green lights flash from Margaret's purse on the passenger seat. She fishes inside and grabs her phone, glowing with new voicemails and texts. She flings it on the seat.

On the interstate, the base of Margaret's neck starts to ache. *Tension headache.* She runs her fingers run over the mole, where the pain is most sensitive. She presses at it with care, the throb building quicker than other headaches. *Goddamn Mom. Sending signals through her alien receiver.*

Margaret speeds up, the bruised night sky wide and welcoming above her. Despite the neck pain, a long-missed feeling of freedom bubbles inside her. She wants to keep driving into the night, like she did when she first left New Mexico to move to California twenty years ago, the sound of

Mom's voice chiding her all the way to Yuma. You can only run for so long, Mom always said.

The pain in her neck now feels more like a poking from under her skin. She exits at Palm Avenue in Imperial Beach, lands her van in the dim side service entrance of a Discount Tire to tend to the ache. She flips on the dome light and rummages her purse for her pill box, ignoring her buzzing and beeping phone. Usually a couple ibuprofens will knock it out. No pill box. Only a handful of the little wet naps Mom's always picking up from the casino. *Where are my pills?*

She holds the spot on her neck. She scratches at it, feels the skin break. Not the first time she's done that when she's been nervous or scared or angry with Mom. But Margaret knew it was never a receiver. Just a goddamn stupid mole. Then light, brighter than a thousand flashlights, pours into the rear window van.

Oh, God, not again.

The light brightens, followed by the horn blare of a tractor trailer. She starts the van, moves forward to the back lot. She dives back into her purse, takes out a wet nap, unwraps it, presses it against the mole. She sits back, drops the wet nap in her lap with a drop of blood on it, and starts bawling.

Jesus, she's not a dog some Tijuana family's going to adopt.

The phone quiets. Margaret adjusts the rearview mirror to see herself. She wipes her tears, sees the face Joana and Tina call Mom's spitting image. Not even a hairstyle can change that face. *Yet. Oh, hell. Is she that evil? Under all those stories and stupid sayings and little things that bug the shit out of me, isn't she a good person? I really fucking hope so.*

Margaret sends Eric and the kids a text. "Be home late. Mom needs more Depends."

She takes out the passports, then snaps her purse shut and throws it on the empty passenger seat. She takes the I-5 southbound ramp to Mexico, the Odyssey ready for flight. Her neck ache begins to subside on its own. Breathing a little air into it does the trick. She's almost about to top the van's speedometer out.

She slows, the line into Mexico just ahead. It won't be that bad going back in at this hour. Coming back into the United States, after she finds her, if she finds her at all, will be another story. *Let's just hope to God she's there. Let's just hope she's doing what she always told me to do when they'd leave me at the store: stay right there until we come back. We'll always come back for you. That's why you should laugh it off every time,* mi corazón. *It's only a joke.*

MOTHERS

MONICA IN GEORGETOWN

PIE SISTERS ISN'T packed on a Sunday night, and though I want it to be darker, the place is airy and bright, and the smell of butter and sugar almost knocks you out. On first glance, it's just students with Macs and books, and couples over slices of pie and cups of coffee. Then, toward the back, her dark hair and unmistakable profile jump out. My palms sweat, and they never sweat. My mouth goes dry. Sure, this was Mom's idea, and I'm only appeasing her yet again, but shit, this is Monica Lewinsky.

"Ms. Lewinsky?" I reach, then pull back. No hand offered from the cool invisible bubble that surrounds her.

"Oh, hi." Only a flat acknowledgment of a smile. "Troy?"

"Are you alone?" I say.

Monica shifts her eyes left. A big, bulky brother in plainclothes sits a table away, deep into his smart phone. It would make sense she has protection. The Presidents and their families have it for life. Why not their mistresses? Though Monica, not the taxpayer, must be footing the bill for this guy.

I'm overdressed in a button-down and tie against Monica's modest Gap-ad wear and her detail's gym clothes. Her manicured fingers lace around a latte.

Way back when I wrote for my high school newspaper in Little Rock, our advisor, the lovely Ms. Georgiou, drilled it into me to be a train on a track when interviewing. "They're giving you *their* time. Don't waste it," she'd say. I had brought that into my budding journalism career in D.C., had it wired in me for years, but right now, it won't work. My skin is shriveling up into itself.

Monica gives me the flat smile again, takes the lead.

"I typically don't meet with strangers, or discuss the Clintons, but the story you told my publicist sounded—provocative. And you were persistent, she said. We were beginning to think we might need to press charges."

I about sink to the floor. Have I been that pushy? I get it from Mom.

"Well, thank you for meeting me. Especially here, in D.C. I'm sure it's the last place—"

She waves it off. "I happened to be here for a fundraiser. It all lined up." She waits, but I'm still speechless. Here's Monica Lewinsky, not that much older than me, both of us merely children in the summer or '98, both of us starry-eyed for the man that would never love us back. She: *that woman*, publicly shamed, and me, her lover's illegitimate black son, waiting, plotting to come forward.

"So," she says, "you claim your mother had a liaison with President Clinton?"

According to Mom, it was back in 1978 in Arkansas. Nine months later, me. I've told her a million times it would make a much sexier story if she came forward first, Clinton's secret black mistress, and then me, the product of that affair, but she's chicken. She's been putting me up to this since I first came out here for college.

"Well, he was just elected Governor of Arkansas then." I lick my lips, trying to get my mouth to move again. Monica must think I'm a perv. But wow, she is pretty. "She was a staffer on his campaign."

"And you know, without a doubt, that *he's* your father?" she says. "My publicist says you have proof."

103

"Yes. That's what my mother says." I can channel Mom when I need to. "And here. I have this."

I pull out a folder from my bag and open it to what what Mom has held onto for so long—her "parting gift" of her time with my father. He gave it to her when their *fling* was over. It's a picture of them in the Arkansas Governor's office, his arm around her shoulders, the two of them smiling wide. "Best Wishes—Bill" in his handwriting on the bottom corner. As I pass the photo over to Monica, it somehow loses all the power it had ever had over me. Over Mom. In that instant, I realize it is what it is: just a picture of Bill Clinton and Mom.

Monica adjusts her posture as she takes a glance. She doesn't even touch it.

"This is nothing. It's a picture," Monica says. "You'll need DNA proof."

She sips her coffee, makes brief eye contact with her guard. He gives her an imperceptible nod. This won't last long, I know. The vultures could swoop in any second. I used to do it all the time as a reporter.

"What do you do, Troy?" she says.

"I'm out of work. My paper shut down. Right now, just spending a lot of time at the Libertarian Party office. Getting ready for the election."

"Are you running?" she says.

"One of these days." My palms have stopped sweating, and her face has softened. Still no vultures. "I want to be President someday."

"Oh," she says. "Just like your father." She flashes that classic toothy smile from her intern I.D. badge, circa 1990-something.

"Yeah, just like him," I say, embarrassed. At least that's what Mom has always wanted for me. Our plan has never changed: expose the truth with Monica's help, then use that vortex of fame to topple the Clintons and build my own campaign to be the first third-party president.

Monica's smile vanishes. She moves her coffee aside. "Do you know the full story? Has your mother told you everything?"

"No." Every time I've tried, she changes the subject. Gets testy. Something hurts.

"I mean, it's quite possible she was a victim—who knows? And I understand if she wanted to keep it secret and avoid the humiliation. But you need to know, Troy."

"Yeah, you're right."

"And, please don't take this the wrong way. I'm never one to bash anyone's dreams, but I think a Libertarian president in this country is a long shot. It's a two-party system."

Her bodyguard stands. Monica glances up at him. It suddenly feels like a breakup. No. A straight-up dumping. I've got a fresh one in mind: Deepa Viswanathan. A cute Indian girl from Philly and a die-hard Democrat. She spent one night at my place in Alexandria a couple of weeks ago. We had two more dates, then she dropped me when I told her the family secret.

"No, no, I get it. I just—*we* just thought you could help us. I'm sorry to trouble you. Coming out here tonight."

She leans forward. "Troy, I wish I could do something for you, but this is between you and mother. Face her."

Monica stands. Flat smile. She seems so alone. I know exactly how she feels.

THE OAKWOOD HAS that depressing Sunday night vibe. All the grills gone cold, pool decks dry and empty, and cars waiting to be rocketed back into the Beltway come Monday. It's the time of night you'd want to watch a movie and open some wine with your lady, if you had one.

Whatever happened to Mom on his Arkansas gubernatorial campaign shorted some fuses in her head. That much is clear. What kind of person goes from being Democrat to Green, then Independent, then Republican, then eventually Libertarian? And what kind of person goes along with it, door-to-door, passing flyers, shaking hands, and serving chicken dinners, following along with *her* dream? A good co-dependent son, that's who.

My phone blinks with a voice mail. Must have missed it on the Metro back to Alexandria. It's Mom again. She's frantic. Something about a pain in her left arm and neck. Headache, too. Calling Mrs. Wilson for a ride to the hospital. She didn't have any of those symptoms when we talked earlier, just before I left to go meet Monica in Georgetown.

This might be a false alarm. It wouldn't be the first.

There's no answer at home in Little Rock. I try Mrs. Wilson, our life-long neighbor.

"Hi, Addie. It's Troy. Is my mother okay?"

"Oh hi, honey. Yeah, she's fine. They're just running some tests. She needs to talk to you though. You ready for the phone number to her room?"

Mrs. Wilson's daughter Niki and I used to fool around in our shed growing up. In elementary school, we mostly kissed, and by junior high, we helped each other lose our virginities. Mom and Mrs. Wilson never knew a thing. Kids learn from the best how to keep secrets.

My phone vibrates. It's a number I don't know, but from a Little Rock area code.

I know what's killing Mom in the hospital. Curiosity. She wants to know about Monica. She still thinks she's the girl in the beret. But that girl is a ghost. Monica's a grown woman now. She's not a victim anymore. I shouldn't be either.

A fourth ring. I answer. Mom's out of breath.

"Oh baby," she says. "I thought I was having a heart attack."

"But you're not." *What I'm about to say to her just might give her one.*

"No. I'm—I'm just tired, I guess," she says.

"Are you still lying down? Still comfortable?"

"Yes, baby, thank you." She sounds suddenly all better. "So how did it—"

"Before that, let's clear something up."

"Oh, baby, I feel that pain coming back," she says.

"You're fine, Mom. You're at the hospital. Now, listen to me. I need to know what actually happened with you and Bill Clinton. Did you two have a... *sexual* relationship?"

"Oh, son, I'm in so much pain."

"Mom. The truth."

There's a certain silence between two people on the phone when the conversation temporarily dies. That living breathing person on the other side, regardless of their location, waits for you, and you for them. That absence of sound swallows you both.

"He—tapped me on the behind," she says.

"Is that all? Nothing else?"

"Yes, that's all."

107

"Who's my real father?"

"Oh, honey let's just talk about—"

"Tell me."

"Will Dumas."

"The bus driver?"

"Yes."

Willie Dumas. The older white bachelor all the kids knew, but no one ever thought a second more about. I had known him all the way from elementary to high school. The man who had always asked why I never went out for football as tall and big as I was.

"Why didn't you two ever make it right?"

"It was a different time, son. Black women didn't just have babies out of wedlock with a white—son, just come home. We'll talk it over."

The silence builds solid again. Reminds me when I actually spoke to Monica's publicist. The woman had said, "Yes, she can meet with you. Briefly." In the stillness of the open line, I couldn't speak.

"Hello," the woman had said. "Are you still there?"

"Are you still there, honey?" Mom says.

"No, Mom. I'm not coming home. Not for a while at least. We both need some professional help. We've needed it for so long. I mean, I don't know why you'd keep up this twisted-ass revenge plot with me thinking Bill Clinton was my father. The politics, the story. Why? Why? You know, it's kind of fucked."

"I know, son. I did you wrong. I was confused and scared. Know that I love you more than anything. I always will."

"I have to go, Mom."

"Please call me, baby. I'm so sorry."

"I will. Just give me some time. Bye."

We hang up, and instead of smashing the phone against a wall, a sudden calm stirs up inside me. It surrounds me, like a hug. It's that fear and confusion she was talking about, morphed into the truth you can't ignore. It's holding me tight, rocking me gently.

I've often wondered what it was like to have my father hold me. Maybe like this. But maybe not, because this is the feeling you get when you've known all along you're all you need. Could be why Bill Clinton always got out of the jams he was in. He was always holding on to number one.

My chest expands, fills with the best breath I've ever felt. I could probably grow wings and fly right out of this apartment if I tried. D.C.'s been killing me since the day I got here. It's been 17 years in this dead air, and it's no coincidence I've been thinking about folding it all up here.

Monica's right: there won't be a Libertarian anything. This chapter's over. I've been thinking lately about Boston for some reason. Maybe Chicago. Hell, even California or the Virgin Islands. Just the other day I read that in St. Croix, you drive on the left side of the road, and in certain bays, the water glows at night.

AGONY IN THE GARDEN

EDGAR'S MEXICAN MUSIC blares when the generator rattles to a stop, and all I can think about is how stupid I was to forget my earbuds today. This day, of all days. These guys can't stop dancing and wailing to their music. Something about *diablito*. The little devil.

"*Oye*, Mini-Mikey." Edgar flashes his big white-and-silver smile. "Daddy coming to let us out early today, ¿o qué? Es New Year's, ¡ése!"

I know it's New Year's. Eve. Don't remind me. And quit calling me Mini-Mikey. They used to call me güerro but stopped when they found out I got Desiree pregnant. Like they think one day I'm going to take over Bradford Construction just because I got his only daughter pregnant. I haven't married her. Not yet.

She's been calling and texting all day. My pocket buzzes again. *Call me now.*

"Well?" Edgar says.

"Hold on."

I put my drill down, find a spot away from the music. I dial my voicemail, but Desiree calls in.

"Baby still crying?" Mary Jane wailing in the background answers my question.

"Yes. How soon can you get here?" Desiree says.

"Not until your dad shows up. Did you call the doctor?"

"They said it's probably colic. She won't eat. She won't sleep. I'm miserable."

"Well, just wait. I'll be home."

But it's not home. Not our home. It's Mike and Aurora's home. They installed me earlier this year when I broke the news of our baby on the way—at Olive Garden, like a dumbass. Desiree kicked me under the table, and Aurora almost puked in between her Spanish prayers. I thought Mike was going to right hook me, but he threw a dollar on the table and said, "I'm going to end you," and walked out, pulling Aurora with him. Desiree cried and said she had a plan. Still haven't heard what it is.

"It's just—my mom thinks—"

I don't want to know what her mom thinks. Aurora spends all day at Our Lady of Perpetual Whatever doing what she calls the Lord's work, but she's really just filling Desiree's head up with religious horseshit, calling her all day.

"What, what is it?"

"Sister Francisca's coming over."

"When?"

"Now," she says.

Goddamn it, we should have left that night I almost convinced Desiree. We were going to drop out of our senior year at Granite Hills High (I didn't give a rip about school anyway), and my aunt was going to let us stay in her empty rental in Riverside. It was the best I could come up with.

"No. We're leaving. Pack up. Pack up Mary Jane. We have to go, Dez."

"No. Just come home. Please. My mom said—"

"No—wait, hold on—"

Mike's driving up to the jobsite. You can hear his hair band music a mile away. Sounds like a bad '80s concert rolling down the street. Never blasts that when he rolls up at home.

"I have to go. Your dad's here."

Back at my sheetrock, Mike clangs in with his steel toes and snug Bradford Co. T-shirt hugging his gut. Not the denim button-down he left in this morning. Guy's had a few and is probably going back for more before he has to head home. I would if I could, this close to Pacific Beach and all those bars. Use that fake ID that's been gathering dust in my wallet.

Mike shouts some Spanglish. "*No trabajo mañana.* Holiday. Off. *Proximo día.*"

He turns to me. "You better get your ass home."

Edgar smiles at me and shakes his hand like he burned it on something.

I wave him off, and before I turn back to Mike, the site's practically cleared out.

Mike pops a mint and heads back to his truck. Engine revved and music up, he speeds out.

INTERSTATE 8 EAST to El Cajon is jammed. Worse tonight with everybody headed home so they can get ready and go right back west to get torn down and say good-bye to this year. Chuck calls and I almost let it go to voicemail. Chuck, my last link to the good old days.

"Levi, bro, what's up?" he says. "Countdown's on."

"Already getting started?" I'm stopped at the I-5 interchange. An endless row of red lights stretch out in front of me.

"You're damn skippy," he says. "So what's the word? You partying tonight?"

Dickbrain still forgets I have a three-month-old. Thinks we can just pick up at the last six-pack or bong hit, or to his apartment last New Year's Eve when he let Desiree and I use his room to conduct our business.

"Hey, you there?" he says.

"Yeah, I'm here." Cars move forward. I inch ahead.

"So what are you doing then?" he says. "Clock's ticking."

Music and laughing come from his side of the phone. Now would be the time. I could exit and head to Ocean Beach. Get messed up with those guys.

"No, I'm shitting you, man." He laughs. "I know you got to get home and practice your Hail Marys."

"Fuck off. I have to go."

"Later." Chuck coughs his good-bye. So easy for that guy. Has no freaking idea.

THE CHRISTMAS LIGHTS and the plastic manger scene on the lawn—the ones I put up alone—are on and it's not even dark yet. Aurora's Taurus sits in the driveway, and behind it is another basic Ford.

I park and wait. Do I call Desiree? Have her run out? Throw Mary Jane to me?

Mike creeps up from behind, his work truck calm and quiet, nothing like earlier. And how in the hell did he get here so fast? All timed by Aurora, I'm sure.

Open the front door and Mary Jane's crying. All those candles Aurora never lit are burning. The place feels like a sauna. She sits on the couch with Desiree and this little dark speck of a nun. I've heard all about Sister Francisca—how she came over to counsel Mike and Aurora when they were having problems, or how she came over and gave Desiree the chastity talk—but I've never seen her. She looks like a skinny old grandma about ready to blow away.

Aurora, in her long, dark skirt and festive turtleneck, leaps up and locks the door behind Mike and me. I used to think she was attractive, something Desiree might look like when she got older, but the longer I stay, the less good-looking she becomes. She hugs Mike and kisses his cheek. He nods at the nun. "Sister," he says, swallowing down a hiccup.

"Desiree, hand the baby to Levi," Aurora says.

Desiree, red-faced and teary, hands me Mary Jane. My little girl stops crying the second she touches my dusty green flannel.

"Now hand her back to Desiree," Aurora says.

Mary Jane starts up again.

"And now to your father," Aurora says.

Mary Jane keeps at it.

"Back to Levi."

She stops.

"¿Es mal de ojo, no, hermana?" Aurora says.

"What's that?" I bounce Mary Jane tight in my arms.

"Evil eye," Desiree says. "Mom says you gave it to her."

"That's not true. Come on, Desiree." The door is right there.

The little nun comes up to me, gets on her tiptoes, and makes a cross with her bony thumb on my forehead. "Stay," she says. *"Por favor."*

"No. This isn't necessary. The baby's fine."

"Andalé," she says, and pushes me gently toward Desiree's room at the foot of the stairs. I know *andalé* means

get on with it. Edgar and the guys at work say it to me all the time.

"¿Están listas?" The nun turns to Aurora.

Every night in my room upstairs, next door to Mike and Aurora's bedroom, before I sneak downstairs to spend the quiet hours with Desiree and Mary JIane, I stare at this painting on the wall of Jesus praying really hard. Agony in the garden, Desiree called it. The guy looks so desperate. So wanting something more. I know the feeling. All I want is to get out of here with my family.

Desiree's bedroom is hot and glowing, with the setting sun spilling into the open blinds. All around, lit colored candles flicker: a red one on the dresser, blue ones in jars with the Virgin Mary on the nightstands, a white one with Jesus showing a burning heart on his chest by Mary Jane's changing table, and small yellow ones in saucers everywhere else.

Desiree files in with her head down. Why the guilt has kicked in so hard, I don't know. I wish she was the girl I used to sneak out of this house and have sex with in the bed of my pickup after we put away a bottle of Bacardi. I wish she was the girl who, last New Year's Eve, told me keep going when I didn't have a condom on.

The nun pulls me into the bedroom. Mike's right behind her. Aurora sides up to me and takes Mary Jane. Aurora hugs her tight, her cheek to Mary Jane's, and whispers, *"Tranquilo, tranquilo."* Aurora puts her down on Desiree's bed and wraps her up in a white cloth. Mary Jane screams.

"That's too tight." I reach for her, and a bony hand grips my forearm. The nun pulls me to sit on the bed. I shake my head. Desiree says, between sobs, "Please, Levi."

Mike, Aurora, and Desiree's shadows start to grow in the hot room. On Desiree's dresser, near a cluster of candles, is a glass of water and an egg. The nun starts to pray, mumbling Spanish from her dry lips.

The nun puts my hand on Mary Jane's forehead, nods at Desiree, and points to the egg. Desiree brings it to her, her chin quivering, with tears running down her face. Mary Jane howls away. We weren't ready for any of this.

"Kneel," the nun says. Mike and Aurora get on their knees and Desiree follows. Desiree looks at me and she's crying hard, right along with Mary Jane.

The nun unwraps Mary Jane and undresses her down to her diaper. My little girl kicks and screams, and the nun knows I want to scoop her up because she grabs my wrist, holding me to the bed. With her other hand, she rolls the egg all over Mary Jane.

"Dez, what's wrong?" I ask her.

The nun's prayers speed up and get louder. Mary Jane's cries turn into a moan.

"You're more in love with the baby than you are with me," Desiree says.

Aurora rocks back and forth on her knees, hands clasped. "You see," she says, "I told you. He gave her the *ojo*."

"Give the damn kid a break," Mike says to Aurora.

"So you're on his side now?"

I turn to Mike. Finally.

"Look here, you little shit," he says. "I screwed up just like you, but I did the right thing. I joined the church and married this woman. Before God."

"Am I your screwup?" Aurora drops her head and sobs.

"Is that true, Dad?" Desiree turns away and looks like she's going to puke.

"Everyone in this goddamned house is a sinner," Mike says, not holding back his burp.

Desiree looks over and I say, "What do you mean I don't love you? We're a family now."

"I was going to get an abortion. But then you had to open your big mouth and tell the whole world."

"*¡Santo dios, no me digas, Desiree!*" Aurora wails.

The nun stops rolling the egg and gets the glass of water. In one shot, she cracks the egg on the rim and the yolk plunks down into it. She keeps praying.

"And all this," Desiree says, "to make you happy, Mom."

Aurora doubles over, choking in tears. The dark bun at the back of her head falls forward. Mike looks like he's about to rip the carpet with his bare hands. The nun holds up the glass and studies the floating egg.

"*Silencio. Todos,*" she says.

Mary Jane has stopped crying. Desiree stands and picks her up off the bed. I'm trembling, and I don't do that for just anything. Aurora stays on the floor, tucked into herself, crying, Mike beside her, shaking his head.

The nun walks me outside of the bedroom. We stand in the entryway. The kitchen clock ticks so loud I can hear time marching on. Outside the frosted glass of the front door, the sky is now dark. The nun holds both of my hands in hers and squints up at me. Her beady, dark eyes lock on me, and I swear she gives me the tiniest wink with her right eye.

"You can go now," she says.

Desiree walks out of the bedroom—her eyes tired, but softer. She holds Mary Jane in her arms and looks down at her in a way I haven't seen in a while. The nun tightens her leathery hands on mine, but I let go and reach for Mary Jane. She's alert: her blue eyes, like mine, sparkle up at me. How could I give this angel the evil eye? She's my daughter. I take her and fix my eyes on Desiree. I open the front door. Laughter echoes up and down Figueroa Street. Cars start up. The night is just getting started. Desiree takes my hand, and I pull her over the threshold.

WHEEL OF FORTUNE

Santa Fé, New Mexico – June 1995

AT THE KITCHEN table, the First Lady leans forward to listen to Sister Rosa. The Sister, in tight jeans and house slippers and a faded black Guns N' Roses t-shirt, dark hair up in a large high bun, appears as though she might have just gotten off work, and not from the convent. More like where the First Lady had dinner tonight. Sister Rosa murmurs in Spanish, maybe a prayer. Sister Rosa opens her eyes and sweeps the air in front of the First Lady, so as to tell her to sit back and relax. Sister Rosa closes her eyes again.

Before sitting in the kitchen, while she had waited in the living room, hot from the shelves of burning candles, walls covered in carvings and paintings of the bloody crucifixion, the First Lady almost left. No agony like that in the Methodist church. But still, the imagery grabbed you and didn't let go. It was so blatant. And that's why she had come anyway: for the God's honest truth.

The First Lady had told her aide, "Do not tell anyone I'm coming here. Do not say a word."

Now in the kitchen, the First Lady ponders the payphone behind Sister Rosa's left shoulder: *What would* they *think of me visiting a spiritual counselor? They'd think I was some kind of Nancy Regan looney. Ha!*

Sister Rosa finishes whispering and opens her eyes. Her calm brown pupils bore into the First Lady, and she feels exposed. Surely Sister Rosa would keep her identity a secret. Wasn't there a non-disclosure agreement they could sign?

Earlier tonight, the First Lady had dined at Tomasita's, where they'd built a special room and named it after her. She noted the afternoon sun shining through the glass at the top of the small rectangular space, and the scent of the new timbers—the crossway beams they called *vigas*. The restaurant owners had installed a gold placard with her name above the doorway. No one had ever built a room for her.

After dinner, she had her driver bring Secret Service and her aide to the Walgreens to get her some Tums. The green chile and chicken and fried dough hadn't sat well. And the First Lady was fairly certain the refried beans were cooked with lard. It tasted delicious at the table—just spicy enough—but once in her belly, it felt all piled up in there, and she thought it probably looked inside of her how it looked on the tin plate it was served on.

Sister Rosa blinks herself fully alert. She reaches for a pad of sticky notes at the center of the kitchen table, and peels one off, her moves slow and deliberate.

When the Secret Service had walked the First Lady up to the door, she had expected she'd be greeted by an actual nun. She noticed the nice drapes inside the home, thought maybe there would be a confessional booth where she could anonymously seek guidance.

Instead, a young girl had answered the door, and muted Wheel of Fortune on television. She seated the First Lady on the couch and left her alone for about a puzzle's worth of time. The category was Before and After.

WAL_ LI_E AN EG _PTIAN P_ RAMI_

The First Lady shook her head at the silent TV. *How do these people* not *get it? And why would anyone ever* buy *a vowel?*

The young girl returned and brought the First Lady to the kitchen. The faint and steady whishing of a washing machine emanated from a room beyond the old yellow Frigidaire.

Now, the washing machine stops. The load is done. Sister Rosa takes a small pencil next to the pad of stickies and scribbles a sentence on the note she had peeled off. She sets the pencil back, turns the paper over.

"First, the answers to your first two questions," she says.

When the young girl had led the First Lady to the kitchen, she told her, "Please think of three questions you want to have Sister Rosa answer. They can only be yes or no questions. Think of those questions very deeply and pray on them. Keep praying on them until Sister Rosa comes."

The First Lady had noticed the pad and pencil then.

"May I write them down?" she had said.

"No." The girl turned to walk back to the living room. "Do you want a Danish?" She pointed to an opened package of Svenhard's Bear Claws on the counter.

"Oh, no thank you," the First Lady said.

"Are you sure?" the girl said.

The First Lady shook her head.

"Well, help yourself," the girl said. "Sister Rosa will be with you shortly."

Now, Sister Rosa shimmies her shoulders just a bit. She fixes her eyes on the First Lady. "First question," she says. "Yes."

The First Lady smiles and nods. Another four years in the White House would be great.

"Second question: The answer is yes."

This didn't surprise the First Lady. He was a dirty man and a recidivist. She swallowed and waited for the final answer.

"Your last question," Sister Rosa says. "You've been praying on this one for a very long time. Maybe too long. It might be time to stop meditating on it and try a different question. Or maybe ask the same question a different way?"

"What's the answer?" the First Lady says.

One thing the First Lady's friends always told her: "You're one tough cookie."

More than anything, she hated being called a cookie.

Sister Rosa slides over the Post-it note.

The First Lady takes it, the adhesive on the back sticks to her finger. Sister Rosa's words read:

Once a tyrannosaur, always a chicken.

The First Lady lays the paper down, sealing it to the table with her finger. "Did you just write this?"

"Yes."

"This isn't a fortune cookie answer or anything, is it?"

"No, your question made me think of it."

"But this didn't answer my question," the First Lady says.

"It's not supposed to. It's a riddle. You're supposed to think about it."

"More than I've already thought about it? I've been thinking about this for a long time."

"I know." Sister Rosa stands, goes to the counter. "That's why you came. Here, take this."

Sister Rosa takes a small napkin and wraps a Danish in it. She places it on the table in front of the First Lady.

"I don't want the Danish," she says.

"Yes, you do. Sometimes you don't know why you want what you want. Sometimes you do. Either way, just go for it. Even if you might not get it."

The First Lady stands, considers the Danish. Her stomach is settled now and the sliced almonds and that band of artificial frosting does look good. You don't get stuff like this in the White House.

"I know I didn't answer your question," Sister Rosa says. "We can't answer questions about life and death, or who will win elections."

"Can't or won't?" The First Lady takes out a one-hundred-dollar bill and sets it on the table. The young girl had quoted her $40.

"That's too much," Sister Rosa says.

The First Lady smiles and takes the Danish wrapped in the napkin and the sticky note. She goes toward the living room. Jeopardy is on now. The young girl gazes at the blue screen. She blurts out an answer before the contestant. "Who is Hoover?"

Alex Trebek says, "You are correct."

The girl makes a fist in the air. She mutes the TV again and stands.

"Keep up the good work," the First Lady says. "Your sister?"

"No," Rosa says. "She's my daughter."

"I like your hair," the girl says.

"Thank you," the First Lady smiles. She sees a painting of Jesus above the entertainment center she hadn't noticed earlier. He's in his robes, praying in the garden.

The First Lady reaches for the front door.

"I did pray for you." Sister Rosa says. "I prayed with all my heart and sent you many blessings for today and far into the future, until your dying days. No matter what happens."

"No matter what happens?"

"It doesn't matter what happens anyway." Sister Rosa goes to the First Lady, keeps her from turning the knob. She makes the sign of the cross in front of the First Lady's face.

"You can sit and eat that here," the young girl says. "They'll wait for you, won't they?"

The First Lady had thought about tossing the Danish later, or maybe eating it when no one was watching, in the car on the way back to the tiny Santa Fé airport. Or maybe she'd transport it all the way back to Washington and have it in the White House. But why wait? Why not eat it right now?

"Yes. Yes, they will." The First Lady moves back toward the couch. She sits, takes a bite, turns her attention to Jeopardy. "What's the category?"

The girl unmutes the television. "Presidential History."

OTHERS

APHRODITE'S ISLAND

GARY CRAMS HIS bag into the overhead, feels the burn of other eyes. Do I really need clothes in eighteenth-century Tahiti? Does it exist?

Later, his pilotless ship lands like an egg dropped onto a down pillow. Outside, no one in sight. Only black sand beaches and a steaming jungle.

Why bring razors without mirrors anywhere? And no need for the guayaberas and Reyn Spooners. His skimpiest thing was the black boxer briefs from Lori.

He reads. *Lord of the Flies*. And waits. She'll arrive soon. That was the plan. Once she'd saved up, resigned, put her stuff in storage.

Night fell. Was there a village? Islanders? That Caucasian kid on his ship staring at him: Did he have family here? A history project, probably.

Still, no Lori. Surely it wouldn't take this long. Maybe she had second thoughts; just couldn't leave Ralph and the kids.

Finally cooler now. Starving.

Morning. My God, this clear sky and air. Water like a bath. Freshen up. Find food. Preferably protein. Still avoiding carbs. Debating taking clothes off.

A little too quiet, and maybe not the best location to start over. Why not France in the 1920s? The Wild West? Or the future?

No. They couldn't go ahead. Only backward. It was the only way to make certain they would be together. Must eat something soon. Fish? Nuts?

It's quite possible her craft arrived on the other side of the island. It's time to look. He ventures into the jungle. Sees a native.

The young boy narrows his eyes on Gary. Gary gestures a flying machine. Wings for hands, hands that land. The boy frowns, then runs away.

Gary can't keep up the pace. Should have lost more weight, worked on a tan. Sweaty and sunburned is not fun. Alas, the boy's village.

The Caucasian kid on Gary's flight is there.

"Why are you here?" the kid asks.

"Why are you here?" Gary asks.

"I ran away."

"Me, too," Gary says.

"Life is good here. They give you gifts."

"Did you see another craft arrive?" Gary says.

"Chief HitiHiti's children. They guard it. There, in the jungle."

Gary's guts tumble inside of him. He feels ill.

"What's the matter?" the kid asks.

"Oh, God, she crashed," Gary says.

"You were meeting someone?"

"Which ones are HitiHiti's children? And how old are you, anyway?"

"Thirteen."

Gary was way off. Lori's kids didn't look that young.

"Take me to them now. To the craft. Please."

"Talk to chief."

In HitiHiti's hut, Gary signs the craft again. Begs. Prayer hands. HitiHiti points to a statue. A female figure. The goddess. She looks like Lori.

Gary worships her. Asks HitiHiti to go to her. He must see her. Now. Please. Gary hits his chest, his heart. HitiHiti shouts. Two come.

One boy, one girl, older than the runaway, older than Lori's kids. Chief's Mini-Me children. With torches, they go off into the darkening night. Gary follows.

At the top of a mound, thick with palms, sits the craft. Like Gary's, but a single pod. She wanted to travel in style. Alone.

Chief's kids genuflect, move forward on their knees. Gary follows. Vines cover the rusted fuselage. Chief's kids light a single torch just inside, the door long gone.

In the dim light, a shrine to the goddess with offerings and flowers glows near the cockpit. Gary attempts to stand. Chief's kids hold him.

Moss and lichens grow on her sarcophagus. The profile is unmistakably Lori's. Gary's hips quake, and his breathing stops for a moment. Chief's kids point.

On the wall, their sacred text:

Gare,

I goofed! Set my temporal endpoint at 1666, not 1766. It's been grand. I die a queen!

Love, Lor

Gary weeps. Alone on Aphrodite's Island. Kneeling in his Calvin's, he feels ridiculous. Should have bought a round trip. Chief's kids kowtow. Pray to him.

Back at the village, HitiHiti crowns Gary in bougainvillea, and then leis him in kukui nuts and hibiscus. The villagers kneel. The prophecy has come to pass.

Many years later, Gary, bronzed sinew and dreaded locks, walking with two of his wives, falls to the jungle floor. A dart to the neck.

He breathes his last. Whispers, "Lori." His wives sob over him. The bushes rustle, and out steps pale-faced Ralph, conquistador in khaki. He drops his blowgun.

Gary's wives grasp at each other. The *other* prophecy has come to pass. So begins the wicked era, so ends the innocence.

Ralph steps forward, claims Gary's wives. They attempt to honor him, as they do all visitors, but none will be like Gary. Never like Lori.

Queen, born of an egg on the sea. Shining goddess from the foam. Benevolent in all her ways, sorrow behind her eyes. Modest and patient. Waiting. Always waiting.

HIGHWAY DARK

THE NIGHT BEFORE Oregon State Police Lieutenant Vince Marx's trainee, Rocio Chavez, was killed, the two of them had been on patrol together on Crown Point Highway in Multnomah County. It was past 2 a.m., and they parked the cruiser at the bottom of a hairpin turn outside Latourell to wait for speeders.

"Sometimes it's nice to find these quiet spots," Vince told his young partner. "You can pass a few hours of the night here and not even know it."

"It's kind of creepy," Rocio had said.

"You can't be a state trooper and be creeped out by something, Chavez." He smiled, tried to tap her on the shoulder. She'd been quiet most of the night.

"I'm sorry, did I say something?" he said.

"No. It's just. It's nothing." She exhaled, steaming the passenger window.

"What is it?" he said.

"It's the anniversary of my cousin Ricky's death. The one that went missing in the Cascades last March."

"It's terrible," Vince said. "But it's a damn good thing they finally found him, you know. At least it gave your family some closure."

"Did I ever tell you how we actually found him?" she said.

"Yeah, Search and Rescue. Last summer, right?" Vince said.

"No. I mean, how we knew where he was?" she said.

"Tell me."

The radio hissed and crackled. It had been at least an hour since they heard a dispatcher. Vince turned the volume down.

"My Aunt Teresa had this New Agey friend who suggested a psychic named Cora Henry," Rocio said. "Apparently this lady helps find a lot of missing people.

"Don't tell me you fucking called her," Vince said.

"I didn't. Ricky's mom, my Aunt Ruth, did. I thought she wouldn't, being so devout. But Ruth was so broken up, she said she'd try anything."

"So should OSP hire this Cora person? Maybe she can solve some cases."

"Shut the fuck up, Vince. Listen. My Aunt Ruth begged me to meet with the psychic, so I said okay. I called Cora before I went and she asked me to bring an article of Ricky's clothing, a picture of him—a real one, not a digital image— and a map of where we thought he was. I have to tell you, I almost turned back when I walked up to that lady's house. I felt like I was going to see a witch or something. It was strange."

"Was her house made of gingerbread?"

"No, listen. She saw me in and I was expecting dark lights and a table with a red cloth and a crystal ball, but her place was plain. And she wasn't wearing a scarf or beads or anything. She looked like somebody's homely old aunt: white hair pulled back, a long skirt and long-sleeved shirt—all neutral colors. She brought me to her kitchen table and we sat down and she seemed to study me for a minute. Then she took my hands and started praying the Our Father. Now remember, there was nothing on the walls, no crosses or Jesus art. The place was bare bones. Before I knew it, I was saying it right along with her. All the time her eyelids were half closed, but her eyes were rolling around. We finished the prayer and she asked for the items. She crossed them, like a priest, you know, then ran her fingers over the map and my cousin's picture and his shirt. That's when I almost ran out of there."

"You should have," Vince said.

"Then she put her hand over mine and looked me straight in the eyes. She kept running her fingers over—"

"You're kidding me, right?"

"This is serious, Vince. Listen. She stopped and said, 'I don't feel good.' So then I said, 'What do you mean you don't feel good?' And she said, 'I don't have a good feeling about Ricky.'"

"No shit?" A pair of headlights crested the hill. The driver coasted by them in the dark, right at the speed limit.

The interior of their cruiser went black again. Rocio put her hand on his shoulder. His smirk faded and his throat gathered into a swallow.

"That's when I knew my cousin was dead. Our family was starting to come to terms. But for me—right then and there—I accepted it."

"Then what?"

Rocio dropped her hand off his shoulder and it fell close to his leg.

"She pointed to this little spot on the map, east side of Mount Jefferson. She didn't say anything about it, though. She lifted her finger and said, 'Tell your family to let him go to the light.'"

"Sounds like a goddamned TV show to me," Vince said. "And I thought psychics weren't supposed to tell you the bad stuff."

"I don't know. But Ricky was right where she pointed."

Rocio's eyes welled up. She wiped her cheeks with the back of her hand. Vince stared ahead through the cruiser windshield and relaxed his grip on the steering wheel. His hands fell to his lap and he turned to her. She looked at him, her dark pupils wide and deep.

He moved his right hand down onto hers; his rough palm encased the soft back of her still damp hand. She leaned in and their lips touched long enough for Vince to taste the moist salt of her tears. Another car crested and its high beams flooded the cruiser. They pulled apart and watched the car pass. They sat for a while in the dark and said nothing.

Just before dawn, he drove her to her cruiser and sent her on her first solo ride. An hour later, a drunk driver ran her off I-84 East into a tree.

The following week at the cemetery, cold and wet like the day Rocio died, he hated himself for not telling her the truth. He couldn't deny there had been something there, but that was going away, and besides, it was wrong for a married man to kiss another woman. Certainly a man who had just found out that he was going to be a father. All of his and Beth's treatments had paid off. After three years of trying, one had finally taken hold.

THE WET SPRING began to dry up, though Rocio lingered. She came to Vince in whispers on his voicemails, or on the faces of retail clerks—her unmistakable high cheekbones and dark hair—at Babies 'R' Us and Target, and lately, in between the clipped voices of dispatchers calling out to him on the radio. He swallowed them all down, masked them in the building joy of his and Beth's growing family unit.

One May morning before work, he was in the shower when Rocio said, *Shut the fuck up*, then laughed.

He froze, rubbed the soap off his face. He stuck his head out of the shower and called back. "Rocio?"

Beth, still at home before going to yoga, walked in the bathroom. "I'm ready to talk about it if you are."

He turned off the water, reached for his towel, and stepped out.

"Do you think about her?" Beth said.

"No. I don't."

He walked past her to the dresser, toweling off. "Thought I heard something."

"You can't act like this forever. You've never talked about it."

He put on his shorts and undershirt without looking at her.

"You're not over it," she said. "You're not over her."

"She's gone. End of story. And what do you mean: 'over her'?"

"You two spent a lot of time together. Late nights, same car."

"Are you suggesting we were fucking or something? She was my goddamned coworker. I trained her."

"I don't know." Beth tucked a lock of her blonde hair behind her ear. "I don't know what to think."

"There was nothing between us. And you can help by not bringing her up."

"To the light, right?" Beth said. "Isn't that what she told you?"

"What the fuck?" Vincent wanted to ram the dresser.

134

"You miss her. Just admit it." She reached for him, her chin quivering. She pulled back and rested her hands on her protruding belly. They were going to find out later that week what they were having.

Fifteen years as an Oregon State Patrolman teaches you to never let anything show on your face or your person. It's always about presence. Except when you're not actually inside yourself. Right then, he wasn't whole and he knew it, and falling to his knees on the carpet in their bedroom of eight years was all his body could do. He sobbed to the point of convulsion. His father's death, the gruesome things he'd seen in the line of duty, the morning he saw Rocio no longer alive, the few years he and Beth had tried but hadn't succeeded— which eventually led him to look at other women, and the ensuing guilt that had been brewing—gushed out of him. He grabbed at Beth's legs and told her everything.

CORA HENRY'S HOUSE in Hillsboro was just how Rocio described it. Vince removed his hat and though her home looked small from the street, it loomed large over him now. At the center of the door, stained glass in the shape of three owls glowed orange and yellow in the early twilight. He rang the doorbell again. It finally opened. The bottom brushed over a plain linoleum floor.

The old woman blinked rapidly and peeked around Vince. "Is something the matter, officer?"

"No," he said. "I need your help."

She offered him a seat at the kitchen table and stood by wringing her hands. "It's thirty-five dollars for twenty minutes," she said.

He thought he heard Rocio laugh.

"Pay now?" he said.

Cora nodded.

She took his cash, then his hands. She prayed out loud, eyes closed. The nerves twitched in Vince's neck where he carried all his stress. He retracted his hand to rub it out, and Cora gripped his other hand tighter. She opened her eyes and studied the hand she still held. She turned it over and examined the side.

"You've had two perfect loves in your life," she said. "One deeper than the other."

"How do you know that?" he said.

"These lines right here." She pointed to two small notches on the outer edge of his hand by his pinky.

"Who are they?" he said.

"One you've met. The other one you still have yet to meet."

He pulled his hand away, stood, and faced the owls.

"You're not finished with something. Someone's waiting for you. Go to her," Cora said.

"What if she's dead?" he said.

"She's alive. They're always alive until you tell them to rest," she said.

Vince rubbed his neck. Rocio's cruiser. It was still in impound.

OFFICER RANDALL LED Vince out to the lot of crumpled car shells and smashed windows. It was getting dark out. "This is it. Take a look. Door's unlocked."

The morning of the accident, the dark blue paint glistened with dew. Except for the shattered windshield and its twisted front end, it appeared to be in fine shape. In the dimming light of the impound yard, the cruiser was now covered in a veil of grime streaked by weeks of steady rain. The blue and red lights on top had lost their shine.

Vince opened the passenger door and a stale mix of pungent cleaning chemicals hit his nostrils. He pulled himself inside, sat in the passenger seat, and ran his hands over the cold and brittle leather. He reached up to the shattered windshield, touched the glass with his fingertips, and pushed to see if it had any give. He looked left, where Rocio's body had been, and went to press the radio console. The panel lit up before he turned the power on and the whir and crackle of the radio filled the cab. He shut the door. A voice replaced the vacant hiss.

"Vince. I've missed you so much."

"No. This isn't happening. You're dead."

"Did you want me, Vince? To be your woman?

The radio crackled.

"I thought that night was the beginning," she said.

That night in the car was a mistake. He should have never crossed the line. He imagined Beth—so alive—reaching for him all this time.

"Tell me," Rocio said. The snaps and whir of the radio drowned out her voice.

He ran his finger over the two notches on his hand. One of those had always been Beth. Always would be.

"I had feelings for you for a while. And I miss you. But, I love someone else," Vince said.

The crackle of the radio faded to a low hissing point until it stopped. "Okay, Vince. Goodbye."

The console darkened. He rubbed his eyes and swiped his face. He shook his head. *No. There's no way.*

Vince stepped out of the car and shut the door. Under the yellow lights of the chain-link boneyard, a rush of warm spring air bathed his neck. Over the tops of other smashed cars, the buzz of electricity wakened him. He hit the top of the car with the heel of his fist.

"Goodbye," he said.

He ran his fingers over the grimy gauze of the crumpled body, leaving four long streaks on the passenger door, and walked ahead.

ONE HOT MINUTE

A DOZEN LITTLE Madonnas in petticoats and leather gloves, raving over the inflatable pink guitars and skull-heart headbands, shifted their squeals to the birthday girl, Sophia—four years old today—who had just emerged with Steven Tyler feathers in her blonde hair. The boys orbited the girls, hitting things and each other, and reminded Phil—also known as Ricky Ruckus, who had just arrived at Mitch and Janine's tiny townhouse backyard—of the skinny bed-headed roadies from his days as a would-be rocker: all of them black clad and busy in sleeveless concert tees with tour dates on the back, their dark attire somehow both an advertisement and a uniform. Janine and Mitch, themselves in Queensryche shirts, greeted Phil on the lawn.

"I love the theme," he said. "Should have worn my headdress."

"It's 'Rock 'n' Roll Princess,'" Janine said. "We love our music, what can I say?"

"It's Phil, right?" Mitch said. "Can you play a few Red Hots tunes, I mean, if it's no trouble?"

Of course he could. Before all this, what felt like a hundred years ago, Phil was the front man for So Cal's biggest Red Hot Chili Peppers tribute band.

"We'll see what we can do." In his surf cowboy getup, Phil felt, as he always did just before he stared a private show, like a first-class tool.

"Right on," Mitch said. "Make yourself at home. Grab a beer. Some food. We'll have you over here. Do you need the chair?"

Mitch turned to the kids. "Look who's here! Ricky Ruckus!"

Phil's fans froze and shrieked in delight, including Macy, the three-year-old daughter of Gwen, the neighborhood mom Phil had been sleeping with for almost four months now. Macy ran up to him and hugged his legs. She batted her big brown eyes the way she did every time he came over to their house. "Up, up, up, up, up!" she said.

"All done, honey, all done," he whispered.

A few paces behind her, Gwen stepped forward with her husband, Scott. From the man's stern expression in the photos Phil had seen all over their home, he had imagined Scott as a smallish, egg-headed geek. Yet here, in this stucco-walled garden on a rapidly warming San Diego Saturday, Phil's lover's husband was at least three inches taller than Phil, and the only thing small on him was his nose. The rest of him showed primed fitness and a wiriness most tall men had.

Throughout his life, Phil had leaned on his good looks and musical talents to establish pecking order around other men, but tall brothers—those six and above—always outplayed Phil's just-above-average height.

Gwen stepped ahead to grab Macy. Phil leaned in, eyebrows pitched.

"Hi." He smiled at Gwen, as though she was any other mom.

"Hi, I'm Gwen, sorry—," she said pulling Macy away. She's a big fan. This is Scott. My husband."

Scott grasped Phil's outstretched hand, shook it once. The height didn't faze Phil now as much as the reality that this man, with his own attributes and likely a steady and healthy paycheck, is who slept with Gwen more often than Phil ever would; though, it didn't matter anymore, did it? Weren't they both moving on? That's what they had decided last week during Macy's naptime.

"The famous Ricky Ruckus," Scott said. He tossed back his weekend hair. In the family photos it was combed over to the side.

"Well, I wouldn't say famous," Phil said. "Infamous, maybe."

The line sunk with Scott. Gwen herded Macy away to the children now poking at an earthbound music-note-shaped piñata. Scott drove his hands into his jeans pockets and turned his back on Phil.

SIX NUMBERS IN and the children and parents fell into that mesmerizing state Phil worked toward every time, even back in the One Hot Minute days. It was called making love to the crowd, and, just like the real thing, you could always tell when your partner was truly into it. He'd learned to look past the stonewalled dads and moms having bad mornings at the Tuesday morning Babypaloozas in the park, both types capable of unthreading his vibe. His wife, Kelly, and all the meditation had taught him that. So, it wasn't too difficult that afternoon in the yard to block out Scott, who marched into and out of Mitch and Janine's sliding glass door during the performance, sometimes with a beer, others without.

"Okay, kids," Phil said. "Grab a maraca. It's time for the Pants Dance!"

Phil and his lover Gwen often laughed about the Pants Dance whenever he came over, how they couldn't get theirs off

141

fast enough once Macy went down for her nap. Afterward, he'd hold Gwen naked in bed and stroke her hair. She reminded him of all the girls that threw themselves at him after shows, even when they knew quite well he wasn't really Anthony Kiedis, nor was his band the actual Red Hot Chili Peppers.

After the Pants Dance came the finale, the "Ranch Hand Boogie." The song that built the Ricky Ruckus empire, coauthored by his wife. Without it, he wouldn't be getting booked all over the county, and though he'd told Kelly many times he'd stopped having fun with the whole act, most recently on their vacation down to Todos Santos, Mexico, she reminded him that his talent to energize little kids was a gift.

They had meditated on it at the beach one evening during the Baja trip, and it was there, deep in his breathing, that he remembered what he had forgotten temporarily: He missed Kelly and loved her. He didn't want to lose her for some suburban housewife. He'd had more than a few, and in the end, those secret relationships did nothing for him. They only wrecked things on the other side. Even if the husbands never found anything out, there was still a dusting of bad karma impossible to Swiffer away.

The kids threw their maracas into the bucket and Howled at the Moon. Their attention snapped toward a platter of fluorescent cupcakes carried out by a mom. Phil continued on singing to the remaining parents. "Under the Bridge" and "Breaking the Girl." Phil's guitar playing had improved over the years, especially now that he was a solo act. When he used to play Kiedis on stage, Phil never had to pick up a guitar. Kiedis's only instrument was his body, and so Phil did what he had to do to keep his pipes primed and his abs tight.

Though the money was better doing these backyard concerts, they never generated the post-show buzz he felt after a good Babypalooza. The comedown was like his old days on stage, and as he imagined, like it might be for those women he used to pay for sex, how they, like he right now, would pack up their guitar and props and leave so the partygoers could get back to what they were doing, and not be disturbed by the entertainment-for-hire. Receive it all, he breathed. *Just receive the gift.*

Janine and Mitch came up to him, still star struck.

"Thank you so much." Janine hugged him.

"And thanks for playing those couple of songs at the end," Mitch said. "Nice job on the censor."

"You learn to modify," Phil said.

"Did you get our PayPal?" Janine asked.

"I'm sure it's in there. I'll check."

"Well, thank you," Janine smiled. "The kids loved it."

Phil scanned the yard. The little girls screamed as the piñata was hoisted above them by another dad. Moms stood in circles with cupcakes. Dads with midday beers, eyes bagged from exhaustion and the tiniest bit of alcohol. Phil would never know this world. He and Kelly had decided not to have children a long time ago.

Gwen had her back to Phil. It wouldn't be right to say bye. That last time, as they dressed in a hurry with Macy crying on the monitor and Gwen saying she felt used, was it. Her husband, Scott, had since disappeared from the garden.

Guitar on his back, Phil waved and went through the garage, just as he had come inside. Never as a musician— wannabe rock star or baby soother—had he come in through the front door. Probably better that way.

He crossed the pavement, heating up from the mid-spring sun. It smelled a little like smoke somewhere; maybe another wildfire in progress. He opened his hatch and threw in the sack, set down the guitar. He thought of Kelly for a moment. How they had planned to go to dinner that night in Cardiff. A man's voice called for him. He turned. There stood Scott.

"Hey," Phil said. "Scott, right?"

Scott appeared to fall toward him. Phil moved quickly to the side.

"Here," Scott handed him a cardboard CD case. The *Ranch Hand Boogie* album. "My kid wants an autograph," Scott said, his breath heavy with beer.

"For sure," Phil said. "Hang on." He patted his pants and shirt, then went to the front console to grab a Sharpie. Here again, he thanked God or Buddha or the universe or whomever for giving him another free pass. His luck extended yet again. Just like Kelly always said, it's like a bank account: The more you put in, the more you can take out.

"To Macy, right?" Phil looked down at the CD case with the dancing little farm animals on the cover. His buddy Tony had done the artwork, pro bono.

"You know her, huh? Why don't you make it out to my wife, too?" Scott said.

Phil stopped, looked up. No sooner did he feel his guts twist up, then Scott drove a fist into them. If Phil had had a bigger lunch, he might have thrown up right there. He gasped for air, clutching at anything as he went down to the pavement, almost saved by Scott's right hook to his chin.

He'd been railed like this before. Somewhere in the early 2000s—'06 maybe—when the band was covering songs from *Stadium Arcadium* at the Santa Fe Springs swap meet. Afterward, they were shooting some Makers and doing some blow with the opening act. Words got heated for some stupid reason, something about the opening act getting cut short on stage, or less payment. Phil had hung on in that brawl, unlike he was doing right now.

Scott's solid shoes—not the flip-flops worn by the other dads at the party—met Phil's face, stomach, shoulders, and groin. Scott continued to pummel him, and Phil let him. The second half of Kelly's gift mantra, which they had reviewed in Todos Santos, was to surrender to giving. You can't *take* your whole life, Kelly said. Come to think of it, the blue sky behind Scott's scrunched-up face now fading, Phil knew he'd been on the take his whole life. You had to give up everything, and now was that moment. He lied back and let the punches come.

"Come on, asshole! Do something." Scott threw another solid one into Phil's face, no longer young and chiseled. He'd let a small patch of fuzz grow in on his chin to try to look more paternal. He'd cut his long hair years ago.

He tasted blood in his mouth with the "Bye-Bye, Night-Night Song" swirling inside his scrambled head. One afternoon, before Macy's nap, he sang it to her, its chords lulling her away to slumber, and as he finished, her sleeping angelic face killed him. He couldn't let her go on being confused about who was the man of the house anymore. All little girls tell their daddies everything, and it was only a matter of time.

Phil swallowed down what he could and turned his head away from one of Scott's jabs. He blinked up at the man and said, "I'm sorry."

Scott got up off his knees and threw the CD down at Phil. He staggered away, toward the opening front door of the townhouse. Two women and a little girl rushed out toward Phil in the street. Screams poured into his hollowed-out ears. The little Madonna's eyes welled and she placed a hand on Ricky's red gingham shirt. Her mother pulled her back.

145

"It's okay," she said. "It's okay. That's not for real. It's just for pretend. Ricky's fine. He's just fine."

The mom turned and looked back up at her friend.

"Are you okay?" she asked Phil.

Blinking, he nodded. "I might need an ice pack," he said. "And please call my wife."

The young girl took off her headband and crowned Phil's head.

"Careful," her mother said.

The little girl whimpered at his condition as her mother tried to pull her away to turn back to the house.

Phil reached up for the girl, her silver silhouette still etched in his puffed eyes. The fans of his heyday were such throwaways. Already grown and corrupted, just like him. These fans, like Kelly said, were indeed a gift. They were so tender and gentle, and they *got* the music. They let it "Wiggle and Jiggle" into their little bodies with no one to judge or reprimand them. He would sing to them forever and not fight it. This, his throbbing body, sealed it. And he'd quit wrecking the delicate and precious lives of women and children, once and for all. Fix his small fans, and himself, before they all went bad together.

THE BIG NIGHT

DR. ADAM FLORES opens Group Session with his standard line: "Good evening, ladies and gentlemen, it's sweet and sour time."

Everyone goes around the circle and says a positive thing about him or herself, then a negative thing. The sour builds, like little snowflakes, until there's a snowball of sorrow rolling around the group. That's how the producers like it. They encourage any and all emotional outbursts. Crying is key.

"What about you, Blitzen?" Dr. Flores says. The cameras swarm toward Blitzen, his head turbaned with bandages, antlers chipped, a patch over his eye.

"I guess I'm pretty funny," Blitzen says.

"That's good." Flores jots a note. "I think you are too."

"Bad thing is, I don't know when to stop."

"Meaning?" Flores says.

"Well, the first time I did the powder, it was like, 'Wowza!' It shot right to my brain. Made me want to, like, snort the whole bag. Good thing we didn't have it all the time."

"Harv, you're nodding. Care to add something?" Flores says.

The cameras turn to Harv. He stretches his still-intact neck side to side. His fractured left arm is slung close to his chest, and his casted left shin is raised up in the elf-sized wheelchair. It's only been three weeks since he and Blitzen fell from the sky over Norway, coked up and on the run, the sleigh plummeting from the heavens.

147

"We didn't have steady access to what you guys have down here," Harv says. "We went bananas for things like cigarettes, let alone the hard stuff. Claus controlled everything. He was the biggest fiend of all."

"Exactly," Blitzen says.

"But was it Claus who created *your* addictive behaviors?" Flores taps his clipboard.

"I used to blame my mother." Jana Tanner chews a cuticle. The cameras swing to her.

"Elaborate." Flores shifts toward Jana's bleached-blonde hair and freckled face.

"She took me everywhere—to all my auditions and stuff—and then when I started making it, she locked me down. That's when I went wild."

"Was she trying to hurt you?" Flores says.

"She was trying to help me. She wanted to protect me." Jana cries. A producer off-camera gives her a thumbs-up, and Jana really lets it go.

"Cry it out, girl, cry it out." T-Wayne Twain smooths the back of her pink, terrycloth tube top. The cameras shift to Twain.

"Do you hear this, guys?" Flores leans forward. The cameras zoom in on his Clark Kent face. "Jana's saying her mother wanted to help. Would you say Claus was trying to help you?"

"Hell no," Harv says. "He had everyone brainwashed, believing the whole fairy-tale bullshit. Those of us who didn't buy it wanted out."

"Talk about the 'fairy-tale bullshit,' as you call it," Flores poses.

"N.P.'s a corporation, plain and simple," Harv says. "We weren't carrying on any traditions. We were making him rich."

"Those workshop elves?" Blitzen says. "Worst working conditions on the planet. Harv here's lucky he was a stable elf, right, Harv?"

Harv nods, closes his eyes, trying to summon some tears.

Off camera, a producer cues Harv to look at his mobile.

"My Uber's here." Harv rolls his wheelchair to the door, hobbles up onto his feet, then grabs the small crutches. A camera follows. "I have to get out of here."

Cue Blitzen.

"Harv, don't go," Blitzen says.

"Stay, dog," T-Wayne says.

"Just let him go," Dr. Flores says. "Let him have some space."

ONCE INSIDE OF the car, a silver Elantra, Harv recognizes the driver. It's Kaz from *The Uber Chronicles*. This too is choreographed, damn it. Just like when the producers gave Blitzen an eight ball to tempt Harv last week. It would make sense that the only way *Babes in Toyland* could go on is if the stars keep relapsing. And here they go again, waving this driver in front of him. They know Harv's talked about her, how he wouldn't mind meeting a woman like that someday. He just didn't know that someday would be tonight.

"Hey, I know you," Kaz says. "You're Harv. From—"

"Yeah, yeah," he says. "Let's just go."

"Where are you headed?"

"I don't know. Tijuana? The airport?"

"What airline?" Kaz pulls away.

"Virgin."

"I didn't know there were any more virgins left," she says, waiting for a laugh. "In the world, I mean."

"Funny," he says. "Just take me to the train station."

"There's a lot of stairs. You sure you can get up and down with those crutches?"

"I'll manage."

"So you're running away?"

"Yeah, this is the part where I'm supposed to do that."

Their eyes meet in the rearview, and Harv gets that funny feeling, the one that's begun to plague him now that his head is clearing. The feeling that detects real things. It seems down here in the tropics, everyone stresses over what's real or fake. When the real stares back at you, you want to grab it and keep it. He's also a little star struck, seeing her this close.

"You can't run away," Kaz said.

"Why not?"

"People want you to get better. They're cheering for you."

"You've got problems too," Harv says. "I've seen your driving confessionals."

"Oh, I know I do. I'm a hot mess. But I talk it out. It's the only way to heal."

"Alone?" Harv says.

"With friends." She signals, then turns. "That's all anybody needs."

Harv exhales, shakes his head, looking out the window. The neighborhood still sparkles in holiday lights.

"I had a lot of friends up north," he says.

150

"Are you going to miss them?" Kaz says.

"I don't know," he says. "Maybe not."

"So, make new ones," she says. "And enjoy what you've got. Looks like they feed you pretty well. On-demand smoothies? And that sushi machine? Wow."

"It won't last," he says.

"It never does." She turns right again. "That's the beauty of it."

Kaz slows the Elantra and stops in front of the three-story Bel-Air bungalow.

"Wait, where are we?"

"I brought you back."

"I don't want to be here. They're not my friends."

"You have Blitzen," she says.

"But he's a bad—influence."

"Lift him up."

"You're a lot better than Dr. Flores," he says. "He's always telling us to have faith."

"Faith is for fools. It has been and always will be about people. But before you can help others—"

"I know, I know, your famous line. Then you say something about taking care of the most important things: mind, body, and spirit. Then you laugh and say, 'And not necessarily in that order,' right?"

"I've got a fan." Her eyes brighten in the rearview mirror. "Here, let me help you out."

On the curb, Harv looks up at her. She's not a Jana Tanner or the reincarnation of sister celebrities who keep appearing every generation. Those kinds of women are fading,

151

like supernovae. Kaz is a normal woman, skin and bones, aging to perfection, everything real.

"So are we friends?" he says.

She rests a hand on his shoulder. "Whenever you need me."

The funny feeling comes back. These cameras will go away one day, he just knows it.

BACK INSIDE THE house, Harv shuffles into the Confessional at the end of the hallway. All the Celebrity Suite doors, with the comedy and tragedy masks on them, are closed. Everyone is either in bed alone or in bed with each other. That or they're all up on the rooftop deck in the hot tub, shattering themselves. Most likely that.

Before he plops down into the easy chair, Harv turns off the camera in the Confessional. He's pretty sure no one else in the house does that. Attention whores, all of them.

The glow-in-the-dark paint splattered on the black walls makes it feel—just for a jiffy—like The Big Night, when that once-a-year anticipation of taking to the skies was all the dope he needed. For years, Harv believed in his tiny heart that only possibility lay ahead, especially on those nights in the sleigh, piloting the ship alone because Claus was wasted. Harv lived for the slice of cold wind on his face, infinity expanding before him. But the reality of living forever began to eat at him. It grew dark and ominous, and as the seasons turned each year, he tried to kill it with whatever poison he could find. Escape was the only way out.

The aches are subsiding and the fog lifting. If he can stick with the regimen, he'll kick his habits and get out of this contract. He'll find himself a place to live, adapt to all this heat, and finally age like a human. Everyone back up at N.P., now cubicled, will go on processing orders into eternity. Free shipping through November—Gray Thursday the new Christmas.

In the miniature universe above him, Harv tries to find anything resembling a constellation. He memorized almost all in both hemispheres, even when he was loaded, but can't find a single one now. He closes his eyes and breathes. The transcendental meditation has helped, though it takes a long time to get into it, his mind is still so quick, so distracted.

He reaches for his phone. Can't meditate when he's thinking of Kaz. It may have all been for show, to build the drama—as the producers say—but damn, it was the closest thing to hope he'd felt in a long time.

The tap of hooves in the hallway pulls him away from waking the phone. Antlers scrape against the Confessional door.

"Hey, Harv. Open up, it's me."

Four beeps followed by the error tone reassures Harv. The best thing about the Confessional is that no one else's code will work when someone's inside.

"Go away, Blitz."

"Yo, you have to come up to the deck. Things are getting crazy. I have a little treat for you too."

"No, please." Harv breathes. *Faith. Faith. Forget it.* He taps his phone; the screen lights up his face in the tiny dark room.

"Come on," Blitzen says.

"Stay away from them and go to bed."

The hooves back away from the door.

Harv opens his Uber app and types Virgin Airlines into the "Where to?" field.

"Hey, Blitz?" Harv says. "I'll see you tomorrow, okay? Get some rest."

Harv stares at the screen. Dozens of little cars move around near the pulsing needle of his location. They turn and scoot backward and forward. She's out there, somewhere. He wonders which one is her, and if he was to press "Request," would she come back to the mansion? Could they make it happen without the producers? *Faith.* He breathes. *No, not faith. Mind, body, spirit. Spirit, mind, body. Body, spirit, mind.*

"Goodnight, Harvey," Blitzen says.

The hooves shuffle down the hallway. A door opens, then closes behind them. Blitzen is back in his stall, just like the old days, when Harv used to put each of the reindeer to bed. Seems like just yesterday they were so small, fuzzy, and sweet. Their cold noses nuzzling into the hay, drifting off, the silent stars going by.

SONS

THUNDER AND TUMTUM

THE HALF-MOON, NOW stationed for the next hour above the horizon, cast silver flecks on the expansive, rippling pool surface. Fiona had relaxed some since they arrived, and had at last sunk a booty-covered foot into the pool. Out across the water, the empty stadium seats illuminated the perimeter of the arena.

"This tank—I mean pool—is so huge," Fiona said.

"It is, I know," Fiona's dad, Rhett, said. Rhett had brought Fiona here millions of times, even during some of the old orca performances, but likely the kid had blocked all them out. Or maybe, as children do as they move into adolescence, forgot most everything.

"You're not going to get in trouble," Fiona said, "for being out here at night?"

"No, no, it's fine. No one checks anymore," Rhett said.

"Where's TumTum?" Fiona peered into the water. Rhett always loved those curious eyes. She looked so grown up, even though she was just about to graduate high school.

"Are you sure you want to do this?"

"Dad, quit asking that."

"No," Rhett said. "This," and he slapped the water. Though he could understand why Fiona would ask that. When she had first came out as a girl her sophomore year, Rhett's world had caved in on itself. He had always feared that day might come along, and he had tried to accept Fiona for who she was even when she was a—he—when she was his little boy, but it wasn't Rhett's to understand, no matter how much therapy or boxing or travel, or all the things he did to try to run away from it.

When Fiona had begun her hormones, Rhett's acceptance crumbled again, and he started throwing hints and questions at her. *Was she absolutely sure about all this?* It nearly broke both of them. Almost killed Fiona. Tonight was one of the few times in the last few years they had spent time as father and daughter.

Rhett lifted the small whistle to his lips and blew. He slapped the water again, and off to their far left, where the gates opened deep under the surface, the big black and white whale grew in size, rising slowly up to them, lumbering yet graceful, menacing but gentle all the while. Once in front of them, his huge body glistening just under the surface of the water, TumTum popped his nose and mouth out. His pink tongue and row of white nubby teeth contrasting against his jet-black skin suggested an expectant smile, except, upon a closer gaze, the mouth fell back like a chasm, the opening wide enough to fit whatever he wanted.

Fiona spidered backward onto the deck.

"It's okay, it's okay," Rhett said. "You remember TumTum."

Rhett patted TumTum's beak. He tossed a few fish from the bucket at his side into TumTum's mouth. Rhett whistled again, and TumTum rolled on its side. His white underbelly shimmered in the moonlight.

"It's just been a long time," Fiona said. She crawled back to the edge of the pool. TumTum rolled again, lifting its pectoral flipper out of the water. Rhett whistled and the whale waved. The whale quickly rolled back and opened its mouth again. Rhett tossed TumTum some more fish.

"He still does tricks." Fiona smiled.

"We don't call them tricks, remember? They're behaviors now."

Fiona inched closer.

"Remember that time I was sitting over there, in the Splash Zone, and I got so wet Mom had to change me?" she said.

"Of course, I remember." Rhett tossed a fish into TumTum's mouth.

"I loved coming here," Fiona said. "Sorry I haven't wanted to come in a while."

"It's alright." Rhett took a knee, hit the water with his hand again. "You're growing up. You'll be on your own before you know it." His throat tightened up. "I'm going to miss you."

"Dad, I'm not dying," Fiona said.

"I know you're not. It's just, you'll be grown up and you'll start a new life—I mean, that's not what I mean. You've already—I'm sorry, I'm just going to miss these times."

The hold on Rhett's throat coughed up and came out as a bark, the start of his cry guttural. He sobbed for a few seconds and reached for Fiona's hand, but she pulled away.

"It's like TumTum here." Rhett wiped his eyes. "He's the last one. You know that?"

"Yes, Dad, I know. You've told me like a thousand times."

"No, but what I mean is that after this one, there will never be any more orcas."

"There will always be orcas," Fiona said. "The ocean is full of them."

"But not here."

"Whales don't belong in theme parks anyway." Fiona gently kicked the water.

Somewhere along the way, kids pass you. They shoot so far ahead of you, the distance becomes immeasurable. Rhett had seen it from an early age—the kid always had the last word. She always knew something better. When Rhett would bring her to the park to show her the orcas, Fiona said, at around six-years-old, "So all they do is just swim around and around all day in this tank? They look pretty bored. It's kind of sad."

"It's a pool, son. Not a tank," Rhett had said.

"What's the difference?"

Rhett explained, as he always did, but there was also that point where you just tell your kid to lay off, and perhaps Rhett did it more often than he should. Jessica tried to remind Rhett that one day, their son or daughter or whomever he would become, would eventually no longer be theirs, and they would have to cherish all those moments, the tough and gut-wrenching ones, no matter what. Was it horrible—was Rhett a terrible, awful human being for sometimes (a lot of the time) wanting to smack the kid when he talked back like that? These damn kids these days. You can't say a fucking word to them and they fall apart.

"There were some good times," Rhett said, his tears dry. "It's not like we were beating them or anything. We've always loved them."

Rhett leaned over to pat TumTum. The whale waited. Its eyes blinked. Rhett threw TumTum another handful of fish.

"So, did you still want to play?" Rhett said.

He knew it would take time, maybe about as long as it took for these orcas in captivity to eventually die out, for Rhett to understand it all. Whenever TumTum died—it could be next year, or anytime in the next 15 or 20 years, or longer—a period of great sorrow would follow. The park would never be the same. He thought something similar about Fiona, how she would be fully her, and how it would not be a loss, instead a beautiful new beginning. Like when the whales were finally gone, a new era would begin.

"Yeah. I'm a little scared though," Fiona said. "And you're sure it's still safe?"

"It's totally safe. These guys are so docile. Here, feed him some. Get to know him again."

Rhett pushed the bucket toward Fiona. She reached in, grabbed a handful of fish, threw it in TumTum's mouth. The whale's teeth, tongue, and jaw, always ready and waiting.

"Now give him a little pat," Rhett said. "Rub his beak."

Fiona smiled.

"You can kiss him, too," Rhett said. "Remember?"

Fiona leaned in, pressed her lips to TumTum's shining beak.

Fiona's smile dropped and she turned to her Dad.

"Can I ask you something?" she said.

"Yes. Please."

Rhett lived for these rare moments. They came like a comet, and usually, if Fiona was in the mood to share, her words that followed often had the same effect as if the comet had hit the earth. Rhett welcomed the impact, and always braced himself.

"Why did they used to call you Thunder?" she said.

Rhett fed Tum Tum some more fish and blew his whistle, pointing at him to submerge.

"Oh, yeah," Rhett chuckled. "It was nothing."

"Wasn't it like the way you talked or something?" Fiona said.

"We just gave each other silly nicknames when I started working here. Did you still want to get in?"

Rhett's first wife and fellow trainer had dubbed him that. She said he was godlike: those shoulders, arms, and voice.

"It was what Tracy called you, right?"

"That was a long time ago. I was a different man back then."

"Mom told me."

"Figured."

"I always liked the name Spencer. How you used to call me Spenny," Fiona said. "I really thought about keeping it."

Rhett's guts tumbled. His throat seized up again. He'd always think of her as Spencer. He had chosen the name. It was his mother's maiden name. The name had died out with her, the last Spencer. He had wanted to keep it alive and in the family.

"Yeah, it's a good name." Rhett tossed a fish into TumTum's mouth. "Were you going to keep it as your middle? Is that what your Mom said?"

Fiona had stopped coming to Rhett for anything close to the heart. Plus, after their divorce, Rhett heard very little from Jessica.

"I was actually thinking of making that my official last name."

"Are you—are you serious?"

"Yeah. Fiona Spencer."

Rhett didn't hold back this time, his eyes pouring.

"Come on." Fiona hit his arm. "Didn't you say we were going for a swim?

Rhett turned to her, tried to hug her.

Fiona still wasn't ready. She never really was. Rhett's brand of affection had always been a mix of play fighting and force, and she stayed away because of it, long before her transition.

"What?" he said. "I just want to hold you as my s——."

Fiona stepped back. Her shoulders rounded forward and her chest heaved up and down.

The line, Rhett had learned long ago, was very solid and close to Fiona, and when Rhett crossed it, which wasn't often these days—more so when Fiona was much younger—it always ended like this. Tears, and lots of them. Demanding her to be anything else never worked.

"Come here, honey. I'm sorry. Look, come here." Rhett reached for her.

"You don't know. You have no idea." Fiona said, backing up to the edge of the pool. She pencil-dropped into the water, like it was all part of the act. Like the old dolphin shows where the trainers would pull a volunteer family out of the audience—the Barnes from Ohio, say—invite them down to the mainstage to meet the dolphins, the mom, dad, and little girl—it was always a little girl, it seemed—all blonde and beautiful, and then, just as the mom was patting the dolphin, she'd fall in, fully-clothed, head first, into the pool.

The audience would gasp and point, and the trainer on the mic would stop the show. "Ladies and gentlemen, boys and girls—please, remain calm. Remain calm." Cast members and trainers would run to the pool where the lady had fallen in, half-heartedly reaching out toward the treading woman yelling for help. The murmurs and pointing from the audience

162

all stopped as the mom soon shot out of the water, feet perched on the nose tip of a friendly dolphin that had raced up from beneath her.

The mom would do a double somersault into the air in her jeans and long-sleeved shirt, then swan dive back into the pool as the dolphin flipped once or twice on its own. The audience, now in on the joke, oohed and ahhed, and the trainer on the mic said, "Ladies and gentlemen, boys and girls, if you hadn't guessed, that's not Mrs. Barnes from Toledo, Ohio— that's our very own head dolphin trainer, Julie!" Let's give her a hand, and let's give a big hand for the real Mrs. Barnes from Ohio! The little girl's mother, sitting in the front row the whole time, would stand up and wave at the audience.

"Fiona, no." Rhett lunged for her, now gone before his very eyes. TumTum would most likely not do anything. All the old jumps and splashes, saddle and fluke rides, beak-tip flips, were all trained out of them. The hope was that the orcas' predatory nature had washed out.

But who could be sure when they came from two different lineages? There were the ones that lived in large, complex pods that stayed together forever. The other kind were the rogues, solitary apex hunters that spent their life in survival mode, mostly male, living at the top of the food chain. The park's whales were all thought to be of the communal kind, though what if the one that took out a trainer all those years ago wasn't himself an assassin scout? Didn't every animal have such a switch, able to be flipped, no matter what control it may have had over itself?

It was like all those times Rhett let Fiona cry in the store, or the way he mishandled her, being a little too firm with his grip, or play that turned rough; were those the rogue parent's moves? Maybe those little acts themselves were instinctual— the caveman father's way of rejecting its offspring early on.

But there were also those moments when Rhett didn't know how to do anything but love and protect his child, when his instincts overrode his propensity for cruelty. If you added them all up, the column for honoring his child was much higher. Rhett never let anyone push his kid around, bully her, or tell her what she could or couldn't do. When Rhett had gone through a spiritual phase, he used to ask God to please always keep his son protected. He'd later added, "from me."

Rhett dove into the pool, his open eyes stinging in the cold salty water. If this was a prank, Fiona would kick back up to the surface to breathe. If it were the real thing, all she'd do was empty her lungs and sink.

The orca pools had no markings on the bottom and no sight markers on the horizon, except for the metal braces that held up the thick glass walls that face the audience. Maybe Fiona swam out there. Rhett's heart thumped, and he tried to relax his eyes to focus on something, anything. He turned back to look for TumTum, who had vanished in the moonlight.

Rhett blew his whistle to call TumTum back up. He slapped the water. He plunged back down to look for Fiona. He saw a flash of black that was either TumTum's fluke or Fiona's legs. Rhett swam in that direction, toward the center. The motion was so quick, too hard to tell who it was. Rhett's chest tightened. He had to surface for air. He blew his whistle again and cried out.

"Fiona! Come on. Where are you?"

TumTum rose out of the water, glistening and majestic, slow and easy. Rhett had brought home so many plush and inflatable orcas over the years, they could have made an entire shrine of them. Fiona loved them and kept most. She said she always wanted to touch their tail.

Rhett followed TumTum as the whale stopped at the mainstage, again waiting for a fish. No Fiona hanging on to his tail or riding his back.

Rhett screamed again. "Fiona, baby, come on." The cold water on his face mixed with the warm saltiness of his tearing eyes. "Oh, God, please no."

He dunked his head again and scanned below. Still nothing. He lifted his head, then a voice called out to him.

"Dad, I'm over here." Fiona was back on deck, far away from the edge, holding her legs to her chest.

Rhett thrashed through the water toward her. His stomach tumbled again in relief, and he wanted only to take Fiona and hold her close. Back on deck, he reached for her.

"What the hell?" Rhett gasped. "Where did you go? Why did you do that?"

"I just wanted to go in and hold my breath. That's all."

"But, honey, I thought—I don't know. I just...please don't scare me like that."

"It was nothing. I went in and got out. I needed some space. You were in my face."

Rhett pulled Fiona close to him, held her, rocked her. When Fiona was a baby, Rhett would hold her for hours at night on his chest so she'd stay asleep. He was paranoid of crib death, and he didn't want to miss a minute of his first-born. Jessica would tell him to put the baby down and come to bed, but he just couldn't.

"I'm sorry. I'm sorry I yelled. I'm sorry for everything. You're going to be fine. It's all going to be okay, okay?"

"Will you still love me?" Fiona asked.

"Yes. I'll always love you."

TumTum tipped his beak at them.

"Someone's hungry," Rhett said. "Get the fish."

Rhett let Fiona out of his embrace. He'd had a fantasy they'd stay until the sun came up, but TumTum would need to go back into holding.

Fiona picked up the bucket, then tossed a couple fish into TumTum's mouth. The arc of the silver bodies shimmering in the moonlight from Fiona's hand to the whale's mouth—a vision Rhett wanted to keep in his mind forever. He closed his eyes for a second, thought about not opening them, afraid he'd lose it. He opened them to the silhouette of his two beloveds, the moon now higher and further up in the sky.

SAD LAST DAYS

DUSTY'S A PRETTY man, and his wife Roberta, incidentally, has a faint mustache. She's fair-haired, like him, but those wispy whiskers come in a little dark. The two of them match in body size and shape, but it's clear he's the one who gets noticed. His squinty blue eyes hooked me at first, until I got a better look at her. She's quite beautiful, and very fit. They went to go get us a drink, and I was suddenly curious about what kind of underwear she has on.

"All they had was Sierra Mist. No St. Croix or whatever." Dusty pushes a sweaty fountain drink my way, across the Formica tabletop.

"Oh, that's fine. I love Sierra Mist." I wouldn't expect Eagle Lanes to have anything but an imitation soda, let alone flavored sparkling water.

"So how much is on the table here?" Dusty sips from his straw. It's magical what white people can do with their straight hair. His is swept back and flirting with greasiness.

"Regarding?"

"You're going to pay us, right?" Dusty sets his drink down. Roberta bites her lip and bats her eyelashes. She's not doing it on purpose, but I'm distracted.

"What he's asking—what we'd like to know is—" Roberta can't get the words out.

"No, I get it. You want to know what's in it for you. Look: Let me be perfectly clear, if the information is legitimate, if you as a source are credible, we'll pay."

"How do you decide?" Roberta tilts her head. Her hair falls to the side. "Do *you* decide?"

"Maybe this will help." Dusty produces a brown legal envelope and cocks his chin at me.

"I took those with my Android," Roberta says. "I have the phone. Do you want that?" Dusty focuses on me as I look in the envelope. The pictures are golden.

"These will do. And yes, we'll pay."

"How much?" Dusty says.

"I need to hear your story. Do you mind if I'm recording?"

They both relax. Roberta's whole frame loosens, like she's just had a massage. I suddenly want to touch her, like the way I've been touching Gisela, Rodrigo's sister. My baby momma. Roberta turns to Dusty, waiting for the next thing. It's beautiful how she drinks him in. Rodrigo doesn't look at me that way anymore.

I leave the interview and head for Mom's before I go into the office in Boca to write the story. I almost call Gisela. We text all the time now.

MOM'S LIVING ROOM is wallpapered with *National Enquirer* pages. She's circled the stories with my bylines in red. Humberto Guerra. When my aunts and cousins and her friends come over, Mom points to the stories, describes what they're about, like she's opening the curio cabinet and rehashing their origin. She has our coverage of Michael Jackson's death framed—Sad Last Days.

Her turban is off and her bald head glimmers in early evening light. She reaches for me, pulls me into her toothpick arms. It could be any time now.

"*Mi'hijo.*" she points at the television. "Did you know the president's daughter, Tiffany, is going to law school?"

"I think I heard that. Are you feeling okay?" I fluff her pillow. She's watching TMZ.

"I wonder if her brothers and sister like her. Parece que no. *¿Tú sabes?*"

"No, I really don't, Mom. Did you eat?"

"I'm not very hungry." She turns off the TV. "Antonia made me a smoothie."

As long as Antonia's been her nurse, Mom's dropped comments about how nice she is, how pretty she probably looks in regular clothes, how she can't believe she's still single, and what a good mother she would be, being a nurse. And she's my age. Mom's been trying to turn me out since I came out.

There's that awkward silence again, which morphs into an awkward question.

"*¿Como está Rodrigo?*"

Rodrigo. We got married a year ago. It was kind of fast. I met him in a bar (everyone in Miami meets at a bar). He was a dancer and I was—looking. He was fascinated with me being a writer, and I was fascinated with how he dressed and moved. He was only my second boyfriend, and we only dated for about half a year. He's Venezuelan and wanted a green card. He's also only twenty-six. My editor Pancho says I scored with that one, as old as I am. I remind Pancho thirty-five is not old.

"He's fine. He's fine."

"*¿Y la hermana? ¿Y la bebe?*"

169

Mom refuses to call Gisela by her name. She knows it's Rodrigo's younger sister and the mother of our child.

"She's doing well. Only two months to go."

Mom holds her emotions in so well I'm convinced it's why she got sick. She used to make fun of me for crying when I was a kid. *Quiere llorar, quiere llorar,* she'd say, like a little futból chant. She wants to cry right now so bad it looks like she's trying to break down a new gumball in her mouth.

"Mom, what's wrong?"

"Nada. Nada."

She knows she'll miss the birth. It's mean how the universe works that way. Takes one, gives another. But would she really care? She thinks this whole arrangement is against God.

She has no idea, though. She's oblivious to my feelings for Gisela. Shit. I was, too. It's been like nothing I've ever felt. It's like she's Mary and I'm Joseph. We're that little image of mother, father, and child you see in every Catholic church. There's nothing from Rodrigo. He'll only be the baby's uncle, biologically. Maybe he's the angel in this Christmas pageant.

Mom grabs my hand and squeezes. "I hope I get to meet her."

She calls the baby a she, even though we don't know what we're having. That's been Rodrigo's only request. He wants to be surprised. Gisela and I wanted to know right away. I think that was when the bond started. We shared a look at that first ultrasound. And then we started talking about baby clothes and furniture. I brought her food. I rubbed her feet. After the baby shower the *Enquirer* gave us, I drove her home alone because Rodrigo had to be somewhere. I don't know why I put my hand on her thigh and let it stay there. She didn't take it off either. That was smack in the middle of her second trimester, when I began finding myself going to her place after work, telling Rodrigo that I was still on deadline.

"I know, Mom. We'll try to make it, okay?"

She gets weaker each time I see her. I look away and meet Dad's eyes in his Army uniform. He stares back at me from the mantle.

"Your father," she says, "he always wanted more children."

"But the war." I know this story. She always stops right there. Two other things she can't say. Vietnam. Suicide.

I wish we didn't have this fear of confrontation. I shatter people's lives in the pages I write, but I can't even talk to my dying mother. We expect so much from our family.

"Look at me," she says. *¿Qué te pasa? Dígame.*"

And so, I tell her. I tell her how I feel. How something is changing in me.

THE STORY WAS easy to write. Kelly Ripa caught with another man at the Eden Roc. Dusty's a maintenance worker there, and Roberta was enjoying the amenities. She'd noticed the thin, beautiful blonde sipping drinks, scrolling on her phone, and laughing. Men in plainclothes stood about, but there was another man, not Mark Consuelos, in his trunks, helping her disrobe. Roberta started taking the pictures, but she was too far away, so she sauntered over there in her sarong, held her own phone up as though she was taking a selfie.

Roberta captured some good ones: Kelly smiling, Kelly giggling, canoodling. Later: Kelly topless. That was the one that paid. We gave Dusty and Roberta two grand for that one. They were happy. Dusty said something about a jet ski.

Roberta was thanking me over and over, said she was a subscriber. She's a lot younger than the retirees who use their pension checks to buy us.

Pancho says, "Good job. This one's going to sell."

"Kelly always sells. Why is that?"

"They see her every day on TV," he says. "They want to see her fuck up."

"These two were giddy. Like they had just found a trailer full of cocaine."

"Exactly," he says. "Hey, do you want to get a drink? It's slow."

Pancho's been trying to talk to me for a long time. He selectively forgets I'm married.

"Nah, thanks. I'm just going to wrap this up and get out of here. I'm meeting Rodrigo."

"How is he? Baby's coming soon, huh?"

"Fine. He's fine."

"You're lucky, Beto, you know that?" Pancho says. "If we could marry when I was younger, I would have fifteen grandchildren by now. Enjoy what you have, you hear me?"

Pancho doesn't strike me as the sweet old gay grandpa type.

"Okay, goodnight. See ya, *tío*."

I COULD WRITE an entire history of the debauchery of South Beach. A Cuban-American's tell-all. It would be dripping with juice. The drugs, the sex. The infidelity. The promise of the best piña colada. Coldest mojito. I'd use some bomb-ass language, too. Spanish. English. Spanglish. But nah.

172

That's not what I write. I'm a whore right now. Using my gift to write about Kelly-fucking-Ripa.

Every now and then, I realize how much all these beautiful people bug the shit out of me.

Rodrigo's late as usual. It's one of the things I noticed early on. That, and how he never wanted to have deep conversations. I asked him once if he thought we were alone in this universe, and he just shut it down, said he didn't like to think about stuff like that. He's settled a lot, become more like a husband, especially since we decided to have a child. He's been taking classes to become a chef. His dream is to have a show on the Food Network. When I first met him, he and Gisela were sharing a studio and they'd invite me over for these amazing dinners he would make. Follow your talent, I would tell him.

He arrives, comes to our table in the back. Jeremias here at Mambo holds a place for me, knows my work schedule is reversed.

Rodrigo kisses me on the cheek. Not on the lips. Like he's embarrassed.

"How was work?"

"Slow. I'm breaking a Kelly Ripa story."

"Oh," he says.

Normally he'd ask for the *chisme* before it prints.

"How was class?"

He shrugs. We order and wait in silence. We've become the couple at the restaurant that doesn't talk. But this shouldn't be a surprise. It's been awkward for a while. When we set up the baby's room a few weeks ago, we hardly spoke. And we haven't had sex in a good while. I often wonder if he's still dancing. I mean, he still has drawer full of thongs.

The food comes.

"How's your mom?" he says.

"Same. Not much time."

"I took Gisela to dinner," he says.

"How's she feeling?"

"Good," he says. "She told me everything."

"What do you mean?"

"So, what, you're not into me anymore? Do you want her? Do you want women? I can't give you that."

"No, listen. Can we talk? Not here."

"We are talking. Right here." He pushes his plate away. "You explain to me."

"I don't know. I think I'm—I'm not feeling—"

He stands and approaches me. He's done this before when we've fought. He gets pushy and loud, and tries to handle me, but he knows I'm bigger and could hurt him. Now, with fury and tears in his eyes, I think he could really unleash something on me he hasn't before.

"Did you fuck her? Did you get her pregnant?"

"No. No. *Cálmate.* I didn't. You know that."

"But now you're fucking her then? Huh?" He's yelling. "Do you love her?" He slams the table. "Do you love her?"

Jeremias comes over. *"¿Todo bien, chicos?"*

Rodrigo tips my plate into my lap. The black beans, still warm, soak through my napkin into my chinos. He knocks my vodka onto the floor, spits on me, and pushes past Jeremias. I jump out of my seat and Jeremias reaches for me with his towel. Rodrigo is gone.

MOM WANTS TO see me first thing this morning. She's been calling and texting all night. Since she stopped the chemo, it's been a steady decline, but today she seems to have new energy in her voice. I know she's still riding high from what I told her last night. She kept saying, "I knew it, I knew it. I knew you'd come around. I knew you'd grow out of it."

Her room is dim, and she has the TV volume low. She's praying.

"Mom?"

"*Pasaté, pasaté.*"

She's even frailer than when I saw her last night. I take her hand and she doesn't grip back like she usually does.

"I've been praying all night," she says. "God has answered me."

"Mom, it's not like that."

"Not you," she says. "For me. And for our country."

Every now and then, she's incoherent, blending her health, world affairs, etc. She sometimes speaks like she's been reading the magazine too much, which I know she has.

"What is it?"

"Our President will not be impeached. I know it. I just know it."

"Mom, don't worry about that."

"He's a great man, *mi'hijo.* Look at how he carries himself."

"He's a trainwreck."

"I want you to call my family." She grabs my hand and squeezes. "I want them all here."

"No, Mom, no."

"*Sí,* it's time."

175

Mom loved going to casinos. She often played in slot tournaments. She'd poured thousands of dollars into those things, and she'd always say, "Today could be my lucky number." I think the most she ever made was five hundred dollars. It was the thrill of it, she said. The thought that you *might* win. All those losses, she said, she put away in a tiny box along with all those things she didn't want to think about. She ignored them until they went away.

"I really wanted you to meet your grandchild. Bring Gisela," she says. "I want to meet her."

"Things are complicated right now, Mom."

She squeezes my hand harder. "They never get easier."

"What should I do, Mom? Mom, tell me. Please."

She closes her eyes.

"Mom, Mom. No."

She opens them quickly. That had been another way she avoided things. Closed her eyes and breathed. Drove me crazy as a kid. I never knew if she was going to start screaming or crying.

"Some people love you for your heart. Some people love you for your head, and some people love you for your guts. I've always loved you for your guts, *mi'hijo. Tú papa, también.* He was so brave."

Now she tells me. I always thought she thought I was the biggest chickenshit. That was what she called me—what they called me.

She coughs and it turns into a fit. I hold her and give her some water, but she's not coming back from it. I guess they always wanted a tough boy, because I can't cry right now. I haven't been able to in a long time.

"Mom." I hold her, *shoosh* in her ear. I've imagined this before. Doing this with the baby. Holding her and rocking her. That's what this pediatrician sleep expert says in his book I'm reading. Wrap them up like a burrito and *shoosh*. Recreate the womb.

She finally calms down. She puts her hand on my chest and tries to talk, but can't. Her hand loses its strength, doesn't push back. When I would get sick as a kid, she would chide me, say it was mind over matter. Cold washcloth? Go get it yourself. I should just let her slip out of my arms. Or better, squeeze the ever-living last bit of shit out of her. But I can't. I won't. It's just not in me. Goddamned tough love.

LO QUE ME DA EL PODER

TODAY IS THE last day of school and there's no assigned seating in class, and who sits right in front of me? Her. She's in her velvety purple waistcoat again. I don't think I've seen her go a day without it this year. Yesterday, she wore a tan skirt-shirt thing that puffed up around her shoulders and hung high above her knee. No tights or anything, just lots of leg showing. That looked really great on her. Today, like yesterday, she's got the flat brown lace-ups on. If we were going out, and if I had my full allowance, I'd buy her a new pair.

Dad officially cut me down to 20 bucks a week though. Last Monday night after dinner, he told us Goring Biochemix had optimized. Translation: there would be firings. First to go are the big guns, like him. He said be ready for anything: public school, Mom finding a job, letting Marta go.

Marta's the only one who knows about my crush on Lucia. Marta is also who I practice Spanish with outside of school. She's always saying, *"Ya ándale. No te pongas nervioso con ella."* Marta tells me to just ask Lucia out. Why wait, she says. You're children. You have time to make mistakes.

Lucia turns around and says: "Do you prefer Tom or Tommy? I've heard your friends call you Tommy."

"Tom's okay."

Her real name is Lucy. Lucille, actually, but because of this class taught by el maestro más famoso de España Doctor Fontanilla, she goes by Lucia. She pronounces it Lu-thi-a, with the Castilian lisp, or as my friend Alberto from Mexico City,

178

likes to say, "Spain's collective excuse to sound like a country full of *maricónes*."

"I'll stick with Tomás," she says and pulls her long blonde hair back over her ear and smooths it down behind her neck. It smells sweet and spicy. "So Tomás, can you believe we'll be seniors next year?"

"It's crazy." What's crazier is this girl who hasn't given me one look in this class or anywhere else at St. Aug is talking to me right now.

Dr. Fontanilla says we can have *intercambio* with our *compañeros* all period, after we complete one last assignment. He hands out a blank page with one question at the top: "*En la vida, lo que me da el poder es _____ por que _____.*"

"*Completa en total,*" he says. "*Yo queiro una hoja llena.*"

He also gives us a brown envelope each and tells us to write our address on it. He'll mail us our paper in one year.

Lucia has put her paper on my desk and the hair that she smoothed around her neck has fallen free onto her left shoulder, hanging down and creating a blonde curtain behind her face.

"Where to start?" She looks down at the blank paper.

"I think it means, in life *the thing that gives me power is* blank *because* blank," I say.

"I know what it means."

"So what is it for you?"

"*En español, por favor,*" Fontanilla says from his desk. He taps his fingers on his right hand. His left—*la pinza*—is out of sight. It usually is.

"*Pacencia,*" Lucia says.

179

I think about what gives me power and nothing comes. I should say something like confidence or truth—anything to impress her—or at least something noble like patience.

"¿Y tú?" she asks me.

"Money."

"Money?" Her eyes crunch together. I've seen this face when Dr. Fontanilla starts speaking very fast in Castilian Spanish, which is lispy, then crosses over into Catalan, which is Latiny. Nobody can understand him then. Lucia's face isn't confused though. It's mad. Her blue eyes lose their sparkle.

"I mean financial independence."

She makes a *hmmph* sound out of her nose and turns around. Once again, I'm looking at her from behind.

This girl next to me named Dawn watches me crash. She rolls her eyes and goes back to work on her paper. Dawn's stuck up like every other girl at this school. Lucia's not. Just moody. I can handle moody.

Dr. Fontanilla walks over. He holds his grade book with *la pinza.*

"¿Qué tal, Tómas?" he says. *"¿Hay problemas?"*

"No, Doctor," I say.

Dr. Fontanilla's glasses are on the verge of slipping off his nose. He's in a short sleeve shirt, not his usual long sleeve and tie. His thick white hair isn't so slick today.

"¿Y tú, Lucia?" he says.

"Todo bien, Doctor. Señor Dinero aquí es loco," she points back at me with her thumb.

Dr. Fontanilla smiles and walks past.

"¿Señor Dinero?" I say to the back of her head.

She turns around fast and stares me down. "You know what I mean." She whips her head forward again.

"Sorry."

She turns back to face me. "You don't have to apologize for being rich."

"But I'm not rich."

"Whatever," she says.

Lucia transferred in this year. On the first day of this class, she sat alone in the row of desks next to the wall, closest to the door. She was out of the way, but you could feel her in the room. She was excited about something, like bottled up energy.

Dr. Fontanilla introduced himself in English and talked about the course; that it was Spanish IIIA and if we made it to this level, he expected us, after that day, to speak only in Spanish. He waited, and as he looked at us, his face went from very serious to soft, almost sad. He went on to say—exact words: "I have three fingers on my left hand." He held the hand at his eye level and studied it. "It was a birth defect. Please do not be scared of my hand. I invite you to look at it. You can even touch it, if you like."

Lucia raised her hand. "I'll touch it."

Dr. Fontanilla walked to her desk and she stood up to meet him halfway. There was a group-groan mixed with quiet laughter when her hand touched his long middle finger. She tapped the tip of his pointer, then his thumb, like she was counting them. He smiled and offered his hand for a shake. Her left hand wrapped around his and they shook, and it looked like they had just made a secret deal.

Lucia took her seat and Dr. Fontanilla looked at the rest of us with his white bushy eyebrows raised up. Everyone seemed to slump into their seats, heads shaking "no." He introduced his hand to every class he taught, and no one in ancient or recent history at St. Aug had had ever touched la pinza.

Now, Dr. Fontanilla says to finish our work and enjoy the last five minutes. It's been a pleasure and buena suerte. Everyone scribbles on their papers, then shoves whatever else they have away into their bags. With one more class left, we're all about to explode. Why even have a last day of school? Lucia takes her time, looks up at the clock above the door. I need to say something. Now.

I lean forward, get a scent of her hair again. She must use natural shampoos. Oceane always talked about her mom taking her to get her hair stuff at the salon and how she'd never go anywhere else. I always felt I had to put an act on for Oceane. It didn't last long between us. A week at the most.

Lucia's hair is tangled in tiny clumps here and there. She runs her hands through it as if she's brushing it. She finishes writing and I try to write a few sentences about confidence and self-worth.

"Are you going down to the soccer fields after school?"

She turns around and smiles, but not in a friendly way. "I don't think so. All you boys running around flinging shaving cream at each other isn't very refined now, is it?"

"It's just for fun. And only the freshmen get creamed."

"Creamed?" she says. "No thanks."

Dr. Fontanilla looks our way and waves. I think he's calling me, but he shakes his head and points at Lucia. She goes to his desk and he pushes a thick book toward her. They smile and say a few words and Lucia tilts her head as she talks to him, making the blonde curtain. She puts the book in her bag, shakes la pinza and smiles wide, then says goodbye to him.

The bell rings at the same time and she turns and walks out without looking back at me or anyone else.

I throw my stuff in my backpack and push past everyone to go to the door. Dr. Fontanilla waves me over to his desk.

In English, he says, "Well done this year, Tómas. Keep in touch."

"Thanks, Doctor. Have a nice summer."

"*Y tú también.*" He taps his fingers and looks up at the clock. He gives me his right hand, but I reach for la pinza. He gives it to me, and I shake it. He raises his eyebrows and dismisses me with a nod to the door.

The sun is shining full blast in the clear blue sky and everything is glowing, it's so bright. Lucia goes to the concrete benches by the century plants, sits, and flips through the book. Her waistcoat is off and she's wearing a pink tank top.

"What did he give you?"

She holds up a paperback *Don Quixote*.

"It's in Spanish," I say.

"I can read Spanish."

"Dr. Fontanilla likes you."

"Shut up," she says.

"Not like you, like you. I mean he likes you as a person."

"Oh. So you do think I'm a person?" She shoves her hand into her coat pocket and pulls out a white cube and pops it in her mouth. "Want one? It's a sugar cube."

I put my hand out and she reaches in the pocket and pulls out another one. It's sweet, but there's something different about it.

"Where did you get these?"

"Teacher's lounge. I'm so broke I can't afford candy." She sucks on the cube.

The night Dad told us they let him go, he left the table and went to the bathroom. Mom grabbed my hand and her eyes watered up. It wasn't real for me until he came back, and I saw his face all red. He stared me down, but not in a mean way. Just serious. Like he had just told me with his eyes the good life was about to change. Lucia looks at me in the same way, waiting for me to crack. Testing me. She holds me in her stare and makes sure I don't look at her clothes or legs.

"I'm kidding," She smiles, still sucking on the cube. "It's acid. It is the last day of school, you know."

"Wait, are you serious?"

"Relax." She grabs my wrist. "Loosen up."

I keep sucking, swallow down the granules. What if she's not kidding? The most I've done is a little bit of weed and I didn't even like it.

The bell rings and the rest of the kids in the courtyard head toward the open doors. She taps the cover of *Don Quixote* and looks at me again. Her blonde hair is tucked behind her ear.

"I do see you as a person," I say. "I have the whole year."

She stops sucking and moves the cube to the side of her mouth, so her cheek sticks out. "The drugs must be working."

"Are you serious that this is LSD? I've never done LSD."

She shrugs. "I guess you'll find out."

"I felt his hand."

"See, you are loosening up." She turns away, staring off at people moving to the next class. God, her profile is beautiful. "You're just a teeny bit more laid back than all these stiff a-holes."

"Thanks a lot.

"You're welcome." She taps the cover of *Don Quixote*. "Took you long enough."

She turns her hand, palm open and resting on the book.

"What did it feel like?" she says.

I move my hand onto the book, walk my fingers into her loose grip.

"It felt weird. But good weird."

Our fingers lock together and it's like electricity running through me. The classroom doors shut, and no one seems to notice us.

"Are we skipping?" She squeezes.

It's Speech with Mrs. Azzawi. My other class with Lucia. I've loved her presentations all year, always talking about her mom and how she used to backpack all over the world by herself. Mrs. Azzawi's having us give a two-minute impromptu on our summer plans. I don't know what my plans are, and I don't care right now. I don't care that this will be the first class I've ever ditched. I'm probably not coming back anyway to St. Aug, and if I can stay here—never move from this concrete slab—I'll be fine. I squeeze back and feel the heat on my shoulders, my body tingling everywhere. Maybe these cubes are laced. It's so warm out and everything in the plant beds is green and blooming, even the cacti.

About the Author

Taylor García is the author of the short story collection *Slip Soul,* and other stories and essays. He also writes the weekly column, "Father Time," at the Good Men Project, and holds an MFA from Pacific University Oregon. García is a multi-generational *Neomexicano* originally from Santa Fé, New Mexico now living Southern California with his wife and children.

ABOUT THE PRESS

Unsolicited Press is a small press in Portland, Oregon. The team publishes outstanding poetry, fiction, and creative nonfiction.

Learn more at unsolicitedpress.com.

CPSIA information can be obtained
at www.ICGtesting.com
Printed in the USA
BVHW081242301121
622868BV00004B/90